Our Forever Crazy Love

CONTEMPORARY ROMANCE

JENNIFER NOLAN

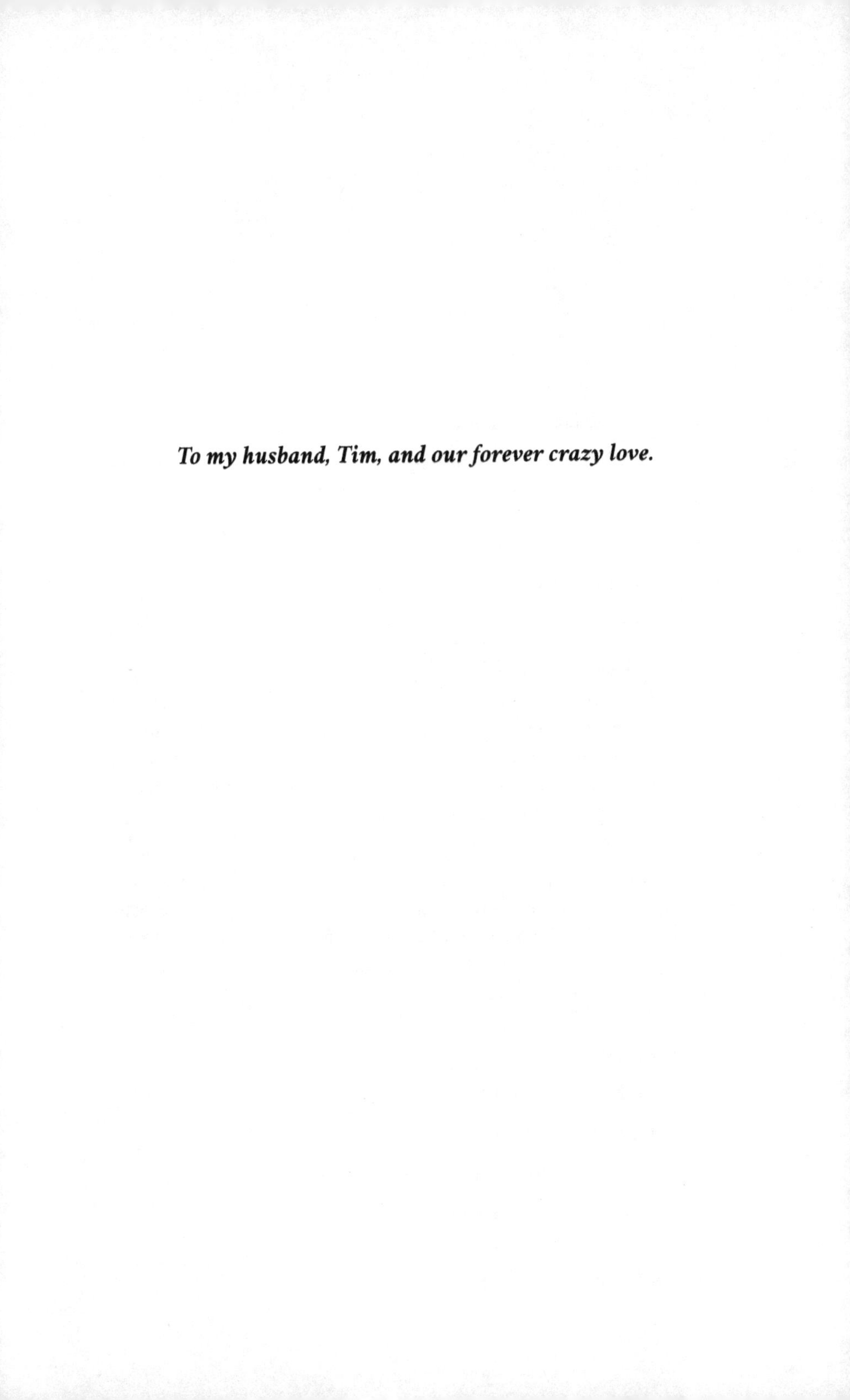

To my husband, Tim, and our forever crazy love.

Our Forever Crazy Love by Jennifer Nolan

Copyright © 2020 by Dunhill Clare Publishing

dunhillclare@gmail.com

First Published May 2020

Edited by CB Moore

Proofread by Jody E. Freeman

Published in Ontario, Canada

Hardcover ISBN: 978-0-9734104-9-5

Paperback ISBN: 978-1-989733-00-4

Ebook mobi version ISBN: 978-1-989733-01-1

Ebook epub version ISBN: 978-1-989733-02-8

Library and Archives Canada Cataloguing in Publication

CONTENTS

Our Forever Crazy Love

CONTEMPORARY ROMANCE

JENNIFER NOLAN

CHAPTER 1

*W*hat if the life we want is waiting for us to choreograph it?

Ten years of waiting and anticipating all ends tonight. I lean forward and adjust the vase of fresh flowers on my coffee table. They were a little off-center, and tonight is too important for me to overlook even the smallest detail. Giving the pillows on the couch one more good fluff, I nod and smile as I look around my living room. *Better Homes and Gardens* would be proud. Ironically, if things go according to my plan, I will have my dad to thank—or blame, depending on how this goes.

It's five past four and the chime on my electronic meat thermometer dings. *Perfect.* Danny will be here at a quarter past four, so that means the roast beef will have a few minutes to sit before I serve it. One final walk through my tiny apartment provides final confirmation; all the details of my plan are in place.

Apple pie is warming on the stove sending the sweet, mouth-watering aroma of freshly baked apples, lightly browned pastry, and cinnamon into the air. Mixed with the roast and grilled vegetables, it's a recipe for the perfect scent. I've laid out all the necessary tools for removing my A/C unit under the window and there are clean sheets on the bed, just in case. I've done everything but put a mint on the pillow.

I spin around in front of the full-length mirror in my bedroom one more time. Even I have to admit, I've nailed this outfit. My new jeans keep it casual but have strategically placed seams and fading to highlight all my curves. My tee shirt looks like I just threw it on, but I shopped online for an hour for this specific one—it's a little sheer, hangs off one shoulder and highlights my lacy blue bra underneath. And even though my toes are freezing on the hardwood floor, I'm barefoot so I can show off my shell-pink pedi. My feet are one of my best features; no way I'm hiding them tonight. I head to the bathroom, check my make-up, and smooth my perfectly styled waves one last time.

It's a quarter past four and I hear the buzzer announcing his punctual arrival. I knew it. Danny doesn't do late. He was never late one day in the eight years my dad was his boss. Yes, his reliability is one of the reasons I crave this man. My palms sweat as I buzz him in so I run them under cold water. Then I use the two minutes it will take him to make it up the stairs to remove the roast from the oven and tent it with the waiting piece of aluminum foil.

I draw in a deep breath, hold it, and then slowly exhale as I head towards the door. But despite my effort to slow it down, my heart continues to race. I do my best to suppress my smile as I open the door. I'm keeping it casual, like he's just Danny moving my air conditioner to storage and not my undying crush finally ready to surrender to me.

He definitely looks laid back; leaning on the door frame, hands in his jeans pockets, looking at the floor. He looks up and shifts the tooth pick to the other side of his mouth, accentuating his perfect bone structure and drawing my attention—once again—to how damn full his lips are. He's five feet eleven inches of yummy. He's always tanned, and his luscious brown hair with soft waves begs for my fingers. I swear I'm already turned on, and he hasn't even said a word. Then he does.

"Roast?"

I regain my composure and nod. "Yep."

He takes a deep breath in and launches himself off the door frame. "Apple pie too?"

"Yep."

He lets out a long frustrated sigh.

What? NO! Not this. Not again. He has a way of brushing me off, and it usually starts with that frustrated sigh of his. You'd think I'd be accustomed to it by now, but it can't happen, not tonight.

He walks over to the window and starts to pull the air conditioner from its perch. It's wedged in tight and the ancient window frame puts up a fight. I silently thank it for making this harder for him. In muted distress, I watch as he takes a screwdriver from my toolkit and uses it to push the frame away from the unit. After replacing the screwdriver in its correct slot—do you see why he's perfect for me?—he shifts his weight, stretches his exquisitely strong arms around the machine, and heaves. I can't help but swoon a little at the way his shoulder muscles flex and settle as he leans the old seventy-plus-pound thing against his chest.

He looks at me, but only to get my attention, and nods toward the door. "Let's go."

My weak smile can't hide my disappointment. Surely he must see I anticipated and want more than this?

I slide on my flip flops, open the door to my apartment, and walk ahead of him down the three flights of stairs to the basement storage area. He's not even trying to make small talk —not asking about my job or my car. Doesn't every guy want to talk about cars? This is worse than I thought.

Of course, there was a chance he would turn me down, but I weighed it as a slight chance. He could still be getting over his divorce, but it's been over a year. She left him; how long can he mourn the loss of that stupid woman? She never appreciated him.

I've written off his reluctance to let her go to the fact they have a son together. That's the only reason I can see for him not moving on to someone better, someone who won't bail at the first sign of trouble, someone with a backbone. Someone like me. I'd never gotten the full story, only bits and pieces I overheard, but I do know that she left him for a guy with more money—a lot more money. She's a member of the Charlotte elite now, a status Danny could never give her.

I fumble with the padlock on the door of my storage locker. I probably should have had it unlocked already so he wouldn't have to stand here holding the A/C unit, but I didn't want to leave it unlocked for too long and I didn't plan on him doing this right away. My roast and pie were supposed to work their magic and slow this project down so it would last until morning or at least a few hours.

With the lock finally off, I open the door and step aside for him to enter the tiny room. I fight the urge to lock him in there and hold him until he wakes up and notices what is right in front of him.

"I didn't ask you to do this, you know," I point out.

He sets the unit down with a grunt and turns to me. "I know." Dusting off his hands, he walks past me as I shut and lock the door.

"I'd already made a deal with the maintenance guy to do this."

He starts back up the stairs. "Yeah, well, your dad asked me to come over here and remove your air conditioner, so here I am. You're welcome."

Damn it. I did sound ungrateful, but this was about much more than an A/C unit. "I made dinner to thank you." We reach the landing with the building's front door and he turns towards it. I can't let him go yet. "You're not staying for dinner?"

"Can't. I've got to go to work."

Puhleeese. What a lame bullshit lie. I know where he works, I know his hours, and I know he doesn't have to go back to work tonight. His shift ended at three and he's not wearing his work uniform.

"Did you change shifts?"

"No, but I've got to go."

He makes a move for the door, but I block him. My anger and embarrassment have me at a loss for words. I open my mouth to speak, but I'm afraid of what might come out. I need time to process this and formulate a response. For once, I have no Plan B because I didn't plan on failing this spectacularly. All I can do is kill him with kindness.

"Take the pie at least. I can wrap it up and you can share it with the other guys on your crew."

"Not tonight." He moves toward the door again, but I block him again.

"Danny, I..."

"Vivey, I told your dad I would come over here and help you move your air conditioner. That's all he asked me to do and that's all I'm going to do." He reaches out and touches my arm as if contact will somehow lessen the blow. "I..." He checks his watch. "I gotta go. I'm gonna be late."

He pushes past me, his size and warmth momentarily engulfing me, his Irish Spring scent lingering in his wake. He doesn't look back as he hurries down the concrete steps and then gets on a motorcycle, illegally parked on the sidewalk. When did he get a motorcycle? He guns the engine, checks for pedestrians and cars, and pulls out onto Drayton Street heading downtown.

I'm not sure how long I stand here, recovering from the shock of that short, excruciating brush-off. I had an armory of temptation in my apartment, and he ran after he caught a whiff of my first shot. I shut the door tight and check that the handle has locked. I love this building, my apartment and this neighborhood, but I'm not naive enough to not be aware of its dangers.

On my way up the stairs, I pull the phone from my back pocket to call Rach; her name is actually Rachael, but I never call her that. She's on standby, waiting for her BFF's sex summary.

She answers. "So soon? Jeez, he's quick on the draw."

"Quick on the draw? Are you kidding me? There wasn't any draw. He moved the air conditioner, then practically sprinted out of here." I plop down on the couch and hug my favorite pink chenille pillow to my chest. It's like putting a fluffy Band-Aid over where I hurt.

"So, start from the beginning. He got there, and then what happened?"

A Rach-analysis could take an hour, fifty minutes longer than the *actual date*. I'm not up for it. "I don't know. He got here, smelled the roast and pie, asked me if that was what he smelled, and then immediately started pulling the air conditioner out of the window. He was definitely on a mission to get out of here. He even lied and said he had to go back to work. He wasn't even wearing a uniform. I mean, what the hell; like I'm not going to notice?"

That shuts Rach up. Danny isn't known for lying. If anything, he could be called too blunt, honest to a fault.

"I need an exorcism, Rach. I need to purge him from my soul."

"I won't argue with you there. I've been listening to you moan and drool over him since you were a teenager."

"I know. I know." I interrupt her because I don't want a review of all the stupid ways I've embarrassed myself over Danny. "Cut me some slack. I was fifteen."

"Okay, maybe when you met him, but this past year...V, if he hasn't made a move by now…" I can tell she doesn't want to say it and hurt my feelings, and she doesn't have to.

"He isn't going to." Ouch. That hurts for me to say. But it's a slap of reality. I need that. I need to move on. "Just give me some time, Rach."

"Sure. Yeah. I know."

A sad silence hangs heavy between us because only Rach knows how hard this will be for me.

I change the subject. "You and your mom going to play bingo tonight?" I know they are. Rach, her mom, and her aunties all play bingo together every Thursday night at their church. "How goes the wedding fund?"

They are all pooling their winnings and saving up for Rach's wedding. She and Luis got engaged about six months ago, it was very romantic. He got down on one knee and everything, but not before seeking permission from Rach's dad. Luis is old-fashioned like that.

"Of course, we can't break our bingo night tradition," she says. "It's growing. Luis's aunt and grandma go with us now."

Rach's family is the opposite of mine: huge and involved. Rach still lives with her mama and siblings and will until she marries Luis next summer.

"Do you want to come with us tonight? The girls will make you feel better. We'll down a few *cervezas…*"

"No, not tonight. Besides, I'm an Irish girl… I've got to drown my sorrows in whiskey. I think it's required."

"All right, you have the night off to drown your sorrows."

"Thanks. And thank you for understanding," I say.

"Hey, I get it. Believe me, I've been here the whole time. The man's smile and body alone could do any girl in. And he used to be sweet to you. Ever since your dad moved away and his divorce, he's changed."

"Yeah, he has. I guess he's only nice to me because of my dad. Now that he's not here…"

"Are you going to tell your dad to stop sending him over to help you? You know he'll do it again."

Damn, she's right. It's a losing battle to convince my dad to let me take care of myself. Half my life I took care of him, myself, and our house, and he still treats me like I'm a child. "Noooo. Oh hell, you're right. If this weren't the most perfect effing apartment in this city, I would move my ass to Sweden and get away from both of them."

Rach laughs. "Then Big Mike would find some dude named Sven and have him at your place taking care of you."

"As long as Sven isn't frigid." We both laugh at that one.

"Do you think that's it?" Rach asks. "Do you think Danny's frigid?"

"Oh, hell no. Like I've always said, there is something about the way he moves. I still can't put my finger on it, but something in his stride tells me he would be a great lay."

"No, no, don't go there. Assume he's horrible in bed and a shitty kisser," she says.

"With those lips? *Yeah, right.*"

Even Rach can't argue with that. "Okay, so he might be a good kisser, but he doesn't deserve you."

"Because?"

"Because he is *estúpido,* a box of rocks. Come on, V; how can he not see by now what an amazing catch you are? You are smart, successful, a gourmet cook, totally cute, and if he ever gave you the chance, I'm sure you would wear him out in bed until he died a happy man."

"I would rock his world."

"Save that for someone who deserves it."

"Like who, Rach? In twenty-five years, I have met one man, *one,* who meets my standards."

"And don't you dare lower them now, girl."

"I'm going to die alone as a cat lady, still looking for that perfect guy."

"No, you're not. There is going to be a guy who appreciates how hard you work to make everything perfect. Did you pour yourself that drink yet?"

I put my phone on speaker and set it on the bar cart in the corner of the living room. "Pouring it now." Rach hears me put ice in a tumbler and pour a generous serving of Jameson over it.

"Of course, you had ice in the bucket."

"And little lemon wedges too," I share as I add one to my drink and water from the pitcher.

"What are you going to do now?"

Rach is my mother hen, a job she and her mamma took over when my mom died.

"Cut the roast into sandwich meat so I can take it to some guys who will appreciate it."

"Okay, good. No single ones yet?" she asks.

Rach is always pushing me to find romance at work which, number one, goes against my policy of never dating at work, and number two, she doesn't know these guys like I do. They are salesmen, always polite, kind and joking, and so full of shit it practically leaks out of their pores.

"No single ones."

"At least Bob appreciates you," she adds.

That he does. My boss, Bob Brockhaus, is the lead salesman in international sales for JetStream Aerospace. He travels the world selling private jets to billionaires and he does a damn good job of it, in great part because he has me. I make his chaotic home- and work-life run like a well-oiled machine and he makes sure I am paid well to do so.

At least I have Bob.

CHAPTER 2

The guys who work in the sales department fit into four categories. DAL: divorced and looking; DAG: divorced and gave up; MAH: married and hanging on by a thread. And finally, CAS: cocky as shit. International sales (I-Sales to insiders) *sounds* cool and sexy, and from the outside might *look* cool and sexy, but it's a lifestyle that is hell on a marriage.

I'm all for confidence in a man, but the CAS guys act far more arrogant than confident. I recall the time we sat around the boardroom table waiting for our quarterly meeting to start and all the CAS guys started comparing watches. One salesman held out his wrist and boasted about the Cartier he'd bought for twenty-six thousand dollars with his last commission cheque. Another tried to one-up him by claiming he'd spent sixty-nine thousand dollars on his prized Roger Dubuis.

Mr. Roger Dubuis turned to me with a sarcastic grin and asked, "Hey Vivienne, what kind of watch do you wear?"

After replying "Timex," I asked, "What time do you have?"

The answer I got back was "9:46."

To which I replied "Wow, how about that! My fifty-dollar

Timex gives me the exact same time and I spent almost sixty-nine thousand dollars less." Mic drop! My response may have been dripping in sarcasm, but he had it coming.

Right now, my boss Bob is in Dubai. He's there at least once or twice a month and stays a few days each time. After three days home, he'll fly to Hong Kong, then Melbourne, and then Seoul before coming home for another three days. He's married... again. Kara is wife number three. He and I are working together to try to hold on to this one.

There are ten different apps I use to keep track of Bob, his travel schedule, his contacts, and his expenses, and almost all are open this morning. He's on a follow-up sales call with a prince, so he had to fly commercial to Dubai. He has enough frequent-flyer miles to buy out first class, but that doesn't immunize him from delays and missed connections.

I'm on line with him trying to find a work around for storms keeping him stranded in Zurich. Kara definitely wants him home this weekend. She and Bob are both hammer-texting me and each other. This is not the first time I've felt like I was standing in a room with them, watching them have a very private argument.

I'm refreshing the Swiss weather site on my main computer screen when Ted Kircher leans in, carrying a heaping plate of my roast beef. He holds it aloft and gives me thumbs up, and I smile briefly at him. I set the carved beef out in the conference room with some bread and condiments when I got in this morning and sent a blast email to everyone in I-Sales to come and get it. None of the DALs, like Ted, will touch the bread. Eating out on the road is hell on a diet, so all the salesmen still looking for love have sworn off carbs. DAGs will take the bread and make a sandwich with the beef and mayo, then add a large slice of the apple pie. MAHs are rarely in the office. If they aren't on the road, they're at home squeezing in all the family time they can.

"This is delicious, Vivienne. Beautiful and a great cook." Ted winks at me as he walks by.

Ted may be hitting on me, but it's hard to tell. Salesmen who sell multi-million dollar jets constantly lay on the charm. Always happy, joking, upbeat, and super friendly. I could take it all as coming on to me, but I choose not to. Not because Ted isn't my type, because he is. I mean, he's tall, dark, handsome and nowhere near as cocky as some of the other salesmen around here.

Actually, Ted is kinda sweet. I felt terrible for him last year when he found his wife cheating on him with his old college buddy. He was heartbroken. Thankfully, it happened early in their marriage before they started a family. Having no kids simplified things leading up to their divorce.

No, the real reason I prefer to believe he's not coming on to me is my rule number one: Don't date guys at work. If I meet them on their level, it all stays completely artificial and friendly from a distance.

I book Bob on the four p.m. train from Zurich to Geneva where he can meet up with Colin, another JetStream sales rep who is there with one of our planes working on a sale. The storms will have moved east of Switzerland by then and Bob can catch a ride home with Colin and be back in Savannah by tomorrow morning.

I text him the details:

*Limo driver on way to frequent flyer club
now. First class train tic in email.
Dinner rez on train (carb free).
Limo will b waiting in Geneva to get to
airport.
Colin will hold flight for you.*

And then soothe Kara's ruffled feathers:

Bob in Savannah office at 6:48 a.m.
Should b home by 8 a.m.
Have a gr8 wknd.

Bob replies:

Perfect, as always. Thank you from Kara
and me.

Kara doesn't reply, but I'm not surprised. She and Bob have been married for almost a year, but she's still getting used to the fact that, for better or worse, I'm part of their marriage. If she wants Bob-time, she has to go through me; I control his master schedule. I get her as much as I can, but seriously, he has to work too.

As I spin my chair around to head for a much-needed pee break, I face Cat, another I-Sales secretary. She's holding the tray with what's left of my roast beef, sandwich fixings, and the empty pie plate and then drops it all in the center of my desk, right in front of me.

"Your stuff was on the conference room table, and I need that table now."

Why does she always make such a humongous deal out of everything? This girl feeds on drama which I do not have the time or patience for.

"Thank you Cat, now I don't have to go and collect these later," I say smiling as I stand and push past her, her cue that this conversation is over.

Technically, as the secretary to the senior sales rep, I am the senior secretary, but it's not a power I use very often. Being a MAH, Bob is rarely in the office so he doesn't need the facilities here. It means I don't have to join in the reindeer games of fighting for conference rooms and supplies.

The latest Bob-crisis has kept my mind occupied all morning, but now the remains of my seduction dinner strewn across the desk take me right back to last night. Before I lose it and go all pity-party at work, I gather up the food and head to the oversized trash bins in the kitchen area. Screw being efficient and thrifty, I'm throwing it all out. Screw saving my plastic serving pieces for another day. Screw my stupid need to have a Plan B and not waste my perfect passion meal—a lot of good all that planning and preparing did me.

I channel my hurt into anger and take it out on the serving platters, slamming them into the wide plastic bin. It feels great and I'm tempted to clean outdated lunches from the fridge for another excuse to throw things. But I stop myself. Ranting at work is unprofessional and beneath me.

As I round the corner near the ladies room, I stop dead in my tracks. There's a guy at the end of the hall in a maintenance uniform. The odds of it being Danny are one in a hundred, but my heart races anyway as I strain to look for his wide-legged, hands-on-hips, Danny-stance. This guy's too tall and lanky. Not him. I want to write my quickening pulse off to anger, but hell, it looks like my heart and hormones didn't get the memo that my Danny-stalking days are over.

My traitor brain joins them, seeing the perfect excuse to call Darlene, my dad's old secretary, to find out why one of her maintenance guys is in I-Sales this morning. After all, if one of the sales planes is broken, I need to know. I mean, this could affect Bob getting home. So, after I finish up in the ladies' room, I return to my desk and give Darlene a call. She'll know if Danny has switched shifts…

"It's one of the new guys," Darlene informs me. "His name's Mark. Why, you likie?"

"No, I just wondered why he's hanging out in I-Sales."

"3-2-B is having landing gear trouble in Morocco. He worked on it last, so they called him in to consult with the repair crew there."

"Oh," is the most enthusiastic reply I can muster. If it doesn't affect me or Bob, I let it fall off my radar. I'm also a little occupied trying to figure out a clever way to turn the conversation to Danny without being obvious.

Darlene knows me too well. My silence is a give away. "He's here. You want to talk to him or about him?"

"About him," I answer and give her the cliff notes version of last night.

"He's still on day shift, sweetie. I have no idea why he would tell you that." She pauses for my reply, but I'm too upset to offer one. "I've got about five hundred other single guys down here. You sure you don't want one of them? Give me your shopping list and I'll send one your way."

I chuckle a little at the idea because I know she's only half kidding. Her desk is the social center of the maintenance hangars. She knows every man and woman who works down there; who's single, who's not and wants to be, and who's about to be.

"I want one who's five-eleven, medium-brown hair with soulful light-brown eyes, full lips, great body, can't tell a good joke to save his life, polite, punctual, kind..."

Darlene lets out a frustrated breath. "Only got one of those and it looks like he's taken by the ghost of wife past. As far as I know, he still hasn't gone on a date since she left." This is going nowhere, so she changes the subject. "How's your dad?"

"Fine," I say. "He and Carla went to the casino last week and he won two grand."

"Wow, good for him. Now there's another one who I thought would never date again. I still can't believe your dad left here to get remarried."

"I know. I was kind of shocked when he signed up for that dating site, then bam, he meets Carla the first week."

"He's one of the good ones. She saw a good thing and grabbed him up."

I sigh. "He is, I know, he's just too overprotective and meddlesome when it comes to me."

"That's love, Big Mike style."

I smile and roll my eyes at her too-true statement. My dad is a bit of a legend on the maintenance floor. He was known for helping people out: giving guys their first job out of college or the military, setting them straight when they screwed up at work or at home. He was the mentor of maintenance. He gave Danny his first job when he was fresh out of the Navy, and even though my dad is fifteen years older than him, they just clicked and became best friends.

"Speaking of love, yours just walked by my window with a pissed-off scowl on his face. It seems like he always looks that way since your dad left," she says.

"I know. I think he's lonely. He needs me, Darlene."

"Maybe he does, but do you need him? I get the hot part, sweetie. Don't think I don't stop and take in the view of him working sometimes, but... I mean... Don't you want someone closer to your age?"

"He's only eight years older than me and no, I don't. I feel like I'm babysitting when I date guys my own age."

"Yeah, I bet you do," she concedes. "You grew up fast after your mom died."

My phone buzzes and I reach to shut it off so I can continue my conversation with Darlene, but it's Bob. "Bob's calling. I need to get this. He's trapped in Switzerland and Kara wants him home now."

"And you are the one person who can make that happen."

"Or die trying. Thanks for the Danny update."

I hang up with Darlene and pick up Bob's call. It's nothing urgent; he's on the train to Geneva and wants to go over next week's meeting schedule so he can stay off his phone once he gets home. Kara has threatened to toss it in their pool more than once. I finish his updates then straighten up the desk to make room for my lunch.

Having lunch alone at my desk is far from unusual. Staying several steps ahead of Bob takes extra effort. It took me six years to work my way from being a receptionist to one of the top secretarial positions in the company. I did it by working my ass off, doing extra work, doing more than anyone could or would ask.

I've been with Bob for a little over a year and I've got my stride now. I know all his likes and dislikes. I know how to get him in and out of all his most frequent sales stops as quickly as possible while maintaining his maximum comfort. I know his diet, seat preferences, shirt size, and favourite tailors.

The other I-Sales secretaries leave together to go out to lunch. I have no interest in going with them. Office gossip wears me out. But maybe I've become too reclusive lately and that's why I can't seem to let go of my absurd crush on Danny.

I'm resolved to take action now and text Rach.

What r we going to b for Halloween this year?

CHAPTER 3

*H*alloween has always been our thing. Ever since Rach and I were little, we would coordinate our costumes and trick-or-treat together. We graduated from candy to liquor prizes in high school but we've always gone out as a team and entered costume contests.

This year, I wanted us to go as Wonder Woman and Batgirl, but Rach put her foot down because we had done that twice already and she hates her Batgirl costume. She wanted to make new costumes and go as Green Eggs and Ham, but I put my foot down on wearing food costumes which are neither cute nor sexy. Besides, any literary reference, even to a children's book, would be lost on the bar crowd. In the end, Rach's mom, Lucca, who is a gifted seamstress, came up with Little Red Riding Hood and the Big Bad Wolf—sexy versions of both, of course. It is the perfect solution.

The fabric Rach's mom used is soft and smooth against my skin, like luxurious satin sheets, only thicker, maybe a rich cotton? My cute red dress has a boob-enhancing corset with hooks in the back, and the skirt is mini-skirt short. It doesn't even make it mid-thigh. I'll want to wear some cute black shorts underneath, or I might be showing off a little more ass than I intend to. When the time comes, I'll slide on some sexy black stockings and killer black heels to complete the look.

Rach will look badass in her wolf costume. It's a full one-piece, charcoal-coloured bodysuit that hugs every one of her voluptuous curves. And all the furry accent pieces her mom sewed on remind me of those little textured pages in a kids' board book you can't resist playing with. I have no doubt she'll be a fierce wolf, quick to draw her claws if anyone, except for Luis, gets too playful with her fur.

While Rach's mom finishes the final details on both costumes, I put myself in charge of creating our agenda. Ever since our first Halloween as over-twenty-ones, Rach and I have had a goal of spending nothing all night, or as close to nothing as we can get away with. It sort of just happened the first year, but we figured out a system (my analytical issues rearing their ugly head) and have it down to an art now. Step One is carrying very little cash on us, our IDs and cell phones strategically placed in our costumes.

Then we start at the Corner Bar near my apartment, home to lots of sleazy old men and no costume contest but extremely cheap drinks. It's my dad's old hangout so I rarely have to pay there anyway. Someone who remembers Big Mike will sit and reminisce about him with Rach and me over a couple of three-dollar drinks. Once we have some liquid courage in us, Rach's fiancé Luis will pedicab us downtown to hit as many costume contests as we can. Even if we don't win the contests, drunk people buy us drinks because they like our outfits. When Luis finishes his pedicab shift at midnight, he'll meet us with his car and drive our drunk asses home—free and safe.

The costumes Lucca made us are awesome. She's the one who taught me to sew... and knit, crochet, macramé, and bake. She's a true Jill-of-all-trades and my organizational idol. She found a tutorial online for making a wolf face with makeup and

Rach sits patiently while Lucca and I touch up details and freeze the edges of her long black hair into a frame around her face. She looks evil and hot. Luis should expect serious scratches on his back later tonight.

We can walk to the first stop because it's close and, well, we can still walk.

The old dudes at the Corner Bar don't disappoint. They buy us cheap shots and throw cliché lines and jokes our way about our costumes. We call for Luis to pick us up at ten so we can head downtown and catch the first contest at the BarBar on W. Saint Jillian Street. Once we hop aboard his pedicab, Rach wastes no time before she catcalls her fiancé as he peddles. "Hell yeah, babe. Look at that ass—dimpled with the promise of pleasure."

Luis laughs and I have to admit Rach is right. His job definitely has physical benefits; the man has some beautiful legs and a butt I don't mind watching for ten blocks.

BarBar is normally a little too young and goofy for my taste, but I need immature and stupid tonight. I love Halloween because being in costume lets me be someone I'm not, someone silly, laid-back, easygoing and fun. Tonight I'm not Vivienne, over-organized control freak. I'm Red, walking trouble.

Rach and I place third in the costume contest behind a girl wearing pasties as a top and some guy dressed as a used tampon (yeah, they keep it classy here). All we win is a bunch of swag from the liquor companies, but it's cool. We trade it for drinks from the college kids who want it for their dorm rooms. While I'm more focused on executing our free-drink, hit-every-contest plan, Rach focuses on finding me a Danny replacement. She keeps pointing out any guy who looks even remotely like he might be my type.

The next bar is more touristy, so there are very few people here in costume which works to our advantage. We win this one and walk away with a hundred bucks. Technically, this could be drink money, but I tell Rach we need to stick to our plan and put this in her wedding fund. I know she's getting pretty tipsy because she hugs and kisses me and keeps telling me what a great fuckin' friend I am.

She doubles down on her search for my next obsession and focuses on a bunch of businessmen who are more than happy to buy us premium drinks on their expense accounts. They're definitely not college boys and one does look particularly good in his suit, but there's no spark there. At Rach's urging, he gives me his business card and I see he works for one of JetStream's vendors. I'm glad I'm in costume and calling myself Red since he is someone I might have to phone for my job.

Rach doesn't hide her frustration. "He was cute!" she yell-slurs at me as we walk to our final contest.

"I know, but he works for HighTel. I have to call them for Bob sometimes."

"So?"

"So…"

I don't have an answer, because she *is* starting to make sense. There are no rules against me dating a vendor. I change the subject, though. I really don't want to go back there. The guy was a good match for me. His only fault is that he isn't Danny, and my defences are down enough for me to admit that I still want the lying bastard.

"Next stop, you have to at least kiss whoever I pick for you," Rach says.

I open my mouth to protest, but she shuts it with a glare. She has great taste and knows me well enough that I'm game.

"Fine, I'll do it."

"Hell yes, you will."

She drags me toward The Rail, our favorite Irish pub and the place where Luis plans to meet up. As we wait in line to get in, Rach makes some needed adjustments to my costume. I've gone from boobilicious cleavage to my nipples almost popping out. I try to stand still as she arranges the laces on the front of my corset, but the cocktails are kicking in and I sway back and forth.

We're in a giggling fit as the guys behind us encourage her to play with my boobs. I start to play with her hair, stroking it, and we move towards each other, looking as if we might kiss. They're chanting "Kiss!" and we laugh, and none of us see the line has moved on. The bouncer yelling, "Move on" breaks our little show. I turn to face the bouncer, fishing my ID out of my top, and stop dead in my tracks.

Danny is sitting on a bar stool in the doorway of The Rail, carding people and looking anything but amused. He holds his hand out for my ID. I'm too stunned to speak. Rach isn't.

"Oh, fuck me!"

She gets several offers from the group of guys behind us. Danny gives my ID a cursory glance because he knows how old I am, and does the same to Rach's, never saying a word to us. He hands them back and looks past us to the next group in line.

"Danny, I—" I begin, but he ignores me and talks to the guys behind us.

"Oh, NO WAY!" Rach won't go through the door now. She's turned she-wolf-crazy Puerto Rican. "You think you can treat my girl this way?" she shouts.

She's in his face. Danny looks up at her slowly and calmly replies, "Get inside, Rachel. I don't have time for this right now."

I push her through the door because my heart is pounding and my head is spinning and my drinks threaten to come up and out all over Danny and the front steps. We retreat to the ladies' room to regroup. Rach shoves me towards one of the stalls.

"Why would you ever want that asshole?" Rach clenches her fists to stop her hands from shaking. "I don't care what he looks like, he's an idiot and a loser."

I only half-hear her tirade. My fuzzy brain finally pulls the missing pieces together so I can form a thought and sentence. "He didn't lie."

That stops her cold. "What?"

"He didn't lie," I repeat both to myself and Rach.

"What are you talking about? So he didn't lie, he just snubbed you AGAIN!" she shouts the last word like she's using it to wake me up.

"No, Rach, he was going to work the other night. He was going to work *here*."

I can tell from her look that she is too disgusted with me to grasp the enormity of what I just figured out. I push myself away from the stall I'd been leaning against and pull on the rickety door handle.

"Where do you think you're going?" Rach pushes the door shut. There is a loud groan from the girls waiting in line outside the bathroom.

"To talk to him."

It's obvious that I have to now I know he's not a liar. Why can't she see this? I pull on the door again and she holds it closed with her hands.

"V, wake up. Whether he lied about the job or not, he totally snubbed you. He's working. He couldn't talk right then. And you think he wants to talk now?"

Damn, she makes more sense drunk than I do. I stew for a minute and then say, "Fine, whatever. Let's just get out of here."

I pull her toward the front of the bar. I can see Danny from where we perch on a window ledge.

Rach follows my line of sight. "You're killing me, V; let him go."

I shake my head and she settles in. She knows I never give up easily.

CHAPTER 4

When Danny takes a break, I approach him, despite the look in his eyes saying he is anything but happy to talk to me right now.

"So, this is where you work at night," I state hesitantly.

He nods, crosses his arms and stands back. He has screw-off body language down to an art, but I'm not intimidated. I know him too well, and drunk Vivienne is ten times more tenacious than sober me.

"Look, I don't know what I did to piss you off—"

He tries to cut the conversation short and doesn't let me finish. "You didn't do anything. I'm not pissed, I'm busy." He looks away like he has somewhere to go.

I know this isn't a good time or place for this, but I want answers. I want a final declaration of some sort. My voice sounds whinier than I want it to. "Danny, I just want to know. I mean, you must have figured it out by now—"

He cuts me off again, changing the subject. "You need to go home, Vivey. You don't need to be here."

Normally, I turn to mush when he calls me Vivey. He and my

dad are the only two people I ever let call me that. Tonight, it pisses me off because it makes me sound like a child he has to correct and then send off home to her parents.

"What the hell? Why shouldn't I be here? I'm twenty-five years old, it's Halloween night, and I can be in a bar if I want to."

He finally looks me in the eyes. "It's late. People are getting stupid drunk and I don't want to have to keep an eye on you. I'll call you a cab."

I'm pissed now; I'm sure my face is as red as my dress. "I have a ride, and I'll stay as long as I want. You don't need to keep an eye on me." I throw up air quotes. "I can take care of myself."

The condescending, patronizing look on his face when he grabs my arm adds fuel to my fire. I twist free from his grasp and walk away but turn and say, "Screw you, Danny," before I'm too far for him to hear.

Rach couldn't hear our conversation, but she can see I'm livid. She pulls me and uses her body to wedge us between two guys so we can reach the bar.

"I'm sorry, V. I really am, but maybe it's what you needed. It's finally over." She talks into my ear so I can hear. She seems a little more happy than sorry.

"He treats me like I'm still fifteen," I shout back to her.

She nods and leans in to talk again. "There's someone here who doesn't think you're fifteen." She turns to look behind the bar and smiles at Sam, my one-night stand.

"Hey, Sam," Rach shouts and waves him over as she nudges me under the bar.

I'm more than shocked to see him. I mean, sure, this is where I met him when he was tending bar six months ago, but I hadn't seen him since or heard from him. Not that I was exactly waiting by the phone. Hell, I don't even know his last name. I've always referred to him as Sam-the-one-night-stand.

It takes him a minute to recognize Rach and me, and I'm a

little hurt—yeah, I must have been really memorable. Then again, he's a cute young bartender I hooked up with on a whim, tons of encouragement from Rach and some liquid confidence from Irish whiskey. He was part of my find-another-guy-and-forget-Danny plan. There's a good chance I'm not the first or last girl to use him for a similar plan.

It's clear when he does place my face and he smiles. I'm relieved.

I smile back. "Hi, Sam. How's it going?"

"Good." He's beaming at me now, and I hope it's because he's recalling our fling. "What can I get you?"

Rach pushes me out of the way; she's clearly on a mission. "V here just got snubbed by this A-hole. She needs a shot of Jameson Black Label and some sympathy." She winks at him. "And I need a shot of Cuervo," she adds.

His eyes ask me if it's true. I shrug and nod.

He pointedly says, "Be right back," to me, then turns to get our drinks.

Rach leans towards me. "You have to kiss him."

I had almost forgotten I agreed to let her pick a guy for me to kiss, but once again she is right. Round Two of the forget-Danny plan with Sam sounds great right now. Even better, let the asshole watch me kiss Sam from his perch at the door—*little girl, my ass.*

When Sam sets our shots on the bar, I let Rach work her magic. She knows that even with a few drinks in me, I'm not forward enough to initiate a lip-lock with Sam.

Rach puts her head on my shoulder and makes a sad face at him. "Too bad there's no one to kiss her and make it better."

He laughs at her blatant ploy but reaches his long arm across the bar to the back of my neck, pulling me in for a very nice kiss. I'm flooded with memories of kissing him before and all the other things we did too. I kiss him back.

The crowd around us gets restless. They want drinks and

their bartender is too busy engaging in a lip lock with Little Red Riding Hood to make them. Their jeers cause us to pull apart. I have to force myself not to look over at Danny. I'm dying to know if he saw and his reaction if he did. Asking Rach is not an option either because she's become a little preoccupied herself by making out with newly arrived Luis.

I get my answer about twenty minutes later. Rach, Luis, and I are still at one end of the bar. Sam stops by every few minutes to wink at me and occasionally kiss me. It looks like we are both definitely up for Round Two.

Luis and Rach pull apart long enough to discuss when they're leaving and whether I plan on sticking around to wait for Sam to get off work. I spot him at the other end of the bar, leaning in, listening to someone. When he leans back, I see it's Danny. Sam looks puzzled, says something to Danny, and they both turn to look at me. Oh, no, he *didn't*! He did not just cock block me. I'm off my chair, pushing my way towards them.

I push Danny aside. Okay, I rub my ass across his crotch and push him back with my hips. I never said I play fair. My eyes narrow as I lean across to Sam. "What did he just say to you?"

Sam looks a little embarrassed when he admits, "He told me you're wasted and I need to leave you alone."

I turn and glare at Danny. He glares back. "What is your problem?" I scream. "Who made you my parent?"

He's in my face and doesn't miss a beat. "Your dad did."

"You and my dad need to get the hell out of my life. You both act like I'm a helpless child. I've been taking care of him since I was a kid. I don't need you to babysit me, I don't need your help, and I sure as hell don't need you screwing up my love life!" People around us stare and try to move away. Danny puts his hands on my hips and tries to steer me towards the back door. I hold my stance and push against him. "Back the hell off, Danny. If I want to go home with Sam and screw his brains out, I will— and there isn't jack shit you can say about it."

There may not be jack shit he can say about it, but there is evidently something he can do. He circles my waist with his arm and lifts my feet off the floor, moving toward the back door. We're halfway there and I'm flailing like a rag doll. My elbow flies into the right side of his head. I'm not very strong, but I'm sure it still hurts.

"Vivey, goddammit, stop it." He sets me down right outside the back door. I step back but only to get some momentum to really slam one into his left cheek. He's as shocked as I am. I've completely lost control.

I hate myself when I do stuff like this. It's like I hold on so tight to everything in my world, and then I get some liquor in me and… Bam! I do something really stupid without thinking. I reach for his cheek, but I can't. I've injured my hand. I curl up around it, moaning and cussing. Danny takes a few breaths to calm down and reaches for my injured hand. I pull it farther under my cape, away from him.

"Let me see your hand, Vivey."

I'm embarrassed and still pissed at him. "No, and stop calling me that." I'm almost crying now, fighting to regain some composure, but the Jameson swirling through my head isn't helping at all.

"I've always called you that."

His voice is calm and softer, his eyes register hurt, and he reaches for my hand. This is nice Danny. This is the guy who's made me laugh and asked about my life and told me really lame jokes and helped my dad with stuff. This is the guy I put on a pedestal ten years ago; the guy I need to let go so I can stop hurting myself.

Luis and Rach are standing in the back door now, watching us. I look up at them.

"Let's go." I turn and walk toward the street, though I have no clue where Luis is parked.

Behind me, Danny calls, "Vivey!"

I don't turn around, but the door clicks shut and I assume he's gone back inside.

CHAPTER 5

*I*t's rare that I travel with Bob, but this week, he's speaking at the JetStream Executive conference in Palm Springs, California. It's a strange event where all of us who work together in Savannah get on planes, ours and commercial, and fly to another location to talk to each other.

Bob is delivering a State of Sales address and the rest of the time will be spent golfing and socializing with other execs. Kara will be there too, doing her exec-wife things. I will be stressing out until Bob's presentation is over, then go along on his golf outing as he's asked me to. It's his way of trying to reward me for all of my hard work, but I don't play and business social events are almost painfully awkward for me. One on one with someone I know I'm great, but in a group of people I barely know and who outrank me by a mile, I'm tortured.

The best thing about this trip is that I get away from Savannah for a few days and will hopefully be so busy I'll have no time to think about Danny and our ugly fight, or Sam and the shambles that is my social life. No better way to do that than immerse myself in presentation notes.

Rach didn't say much on our way home Halloween night or

since. I'm sure she's waiting for my take on the whole debacle. We've talked every day but only about my trip, her work at the restaurant, and her wedding plans. In retrospect, this whole Danny thing has gotten out of control. He was my first crush and yes, that tends to stay with a girl. I was a socially awkward but overly mature fifteen-year-old disgusted with boys my own age.

Not only was he a smokin' hot twenty-three-year-old man, but he talked to me, real conversations, and paid attention to me. That was heavy stuff. The fact he was newly-married with a baby was incidental. In my teenage brain, I fantasized that he would wake up and realize that his wife was an evil hag and that I was the right girl for him. Then it happened… at least the part where she was out of the picture, although she left him—which is more evidence that she's completely insane.

To be fair, I was starting to give up on the whole Danny-and-me idea until she left. It felt too much like fate. I waited a year, and then another for him to make a move, and it's not like he didn't have an excuse to see me. My dad moved to New Orleans to marry Carla about the same time as Danny's divorce. Dad asked Danny to keep an eye on me and help me out—which is annoying in so many ways. He could have called or come by my place anytime. But he didn't.

I've made far too many excuses for him. It hurts like hell to finally face the fact that he isn't interested in me, and alone in my hotel room in Palm Springs I have too much time to think. Hell, I could be anywhere and I'd have too much time to overanalyze the whys and why-nots of me and Danny. I'm actually looking forward to the golf outing as a mental distraction.

*

It is a picture-perfect day as we step onto the course with stunning views in every direction. A warm breeze brushes past my cheeks and the blue sky above stretches out in every direction with an occasional white fluffy cloud floating by. The grounds are manicured to perfection. Towering palm trees and low-lying plants erupting in red, orange, and yellow blossoms line the edges of the fairway and rolling hills basked in sunlight are the backdrop to the clearing ahead.

I breathe in the fresh air in awe of Mother Nature. There needs to be a way for introverts like me to hang out in beautiful places like this without having to deal with other people.

So far, today hasn't been too stressful for me. I drive the cart and manage the snacks for the group. The wives are here, which allows me to fall off the social totem pole and gives me a chance to get to know Kara a little better, although she's mostly busy chatting up the top-exec wives. She really is an asset to Bob. I hope she stays.

I've been pretending to have something engrossing and important on my iPad all day as an excuse not to have to chit chat. Sitting in the golf cart, I'm actually reading a BDSM romance and kind of enjoying mentally jumping between the dungeon with Master Raffe and the golf course. I'm on a particularly steamy part when someone approaches my cart.

"Don't tell me you're working out here."

Oh God, it's Joel Rockhurst! Why is the CEO of the company coming over to talk to me? He's supposed to stay on the course with his buddies and send some assistant if he wants a snack. I smile weakly.

"Oh, no, sir." Then I remember what I was actually doing and close the iPad to hide the book. "Well, a little," I sheepishly admit. "I was just checking the flights for tomorrow."

He nods his approval and holds out his hand to shake mine. "Joel Rockhurst."

"Vivienne Ramsey." It's one of those uncomfortable introductions when you know of someone but don't know them. "I'm Bob Brockhaus's secretary."

He nods again and says, "What have you got in there?" He glances at the cooler attached to the back of my cart.

I hop out and open the lid. "Water, Cokes, Diet Cokes, and Coke Zero."

"No tea?"

"Um, no." I move the ice around as if that will somehow magically make some tea appear. "I could run up to the club house and get you some."

He smiles at me like I gave the answer he was hoping for.

"Sweet or unsweet? Lemon? Sugar? Sweetener?" I ask.

Again, I get an approving smile. "Unsweet with extra lemon, no sweetener."

"Two lemons?"

"Two would be perfect."

I cheerfully tell him, "Be right back" as I start the cart and turn toward the club house. I drive fast, welcoming the chance to get away from him. He makes me a bit nervous. Luckily, once I return and give him his unsweet double-lemon tea, Joel Rockhurst doesn't feel the need to chat anymore, although I do catch him looking at me more than once. When I do, he doesn't look away like he's been caught. I guess you can look at whoever the hell you want when you run the company. I just can't for the life of me figure out why.

It doesn't feel overtly sexual, and he's married. Wife number four is Miss Georgia from three years ago. She's vivacious, stunning, petite—my complete opposite. I doubt our CEO has suddenly developed a thing for quiet, tall, curvy secretaries.

When we reach the thirteenth hole, I make an excuse about checking on arrangements for tonight's dinner and ride off. Not that I have anything to do with planning the dinner, but most execs aren't too interested in what I'm up to anyway. Bob would know I'm lying, but he's engrossed in making sure Kara is having a good time. I'm secretly planning on skipping out on the dinner and taking the rental car to go eat alone at In-N-Out Burger, then find a quiet place near the beach to sit and read my book. It's my true reward for all the hard work.

I convince Bob that I've had too much sun out on the golf course and I'm taking the car to go get aspirin and aloe. It's a semi-valid excuse. I am an Irish shade of pale that's usually only seen on the dead. I've also got red spots on my shoulders where I missed rubbing my mega sunblock.

In-N-Out doesn't disappoint. We don't have them in Savannah; Bob took me to one when we were in L.A. and got me hooked. The dinner I skipped was over a hundred dollars a plate (wine not included) but I am so much happier with my cheeseburger, fries, and shake. My belly is happy and full and the sun is setting when I find a small public park with benches and a view of the ocean. An out-of-the-way bench looks safe, and I get back to my dungeon time with Master Raffe.

I'm more than a little surprised how much this book turns me on. In real life, the idea of being a submissive woman is ridiculous. I've always been smarter and more organized and better at taking care of everyone than anyone I know, especially men. I would no doubt get frustrated if Master Raffe tied one of the knots wrong, since I'd have to show him how to properly tie the ropes (as I would have thoroughly researched and practiced beforehand). And I would probably end up buying everything for our dungeon time because I can out-shop all humans.

Eventually, I would end up in charge—again. It always happens that way. It can be a great thing, like at work where I get paid extremely well for it. Or it can be an annoying thing, like at home where I did everything and my dad still treated me like I was feeble-minded and couldn't function without him.

I stop overanalyzing (at least for a minute) and let myself enjoy being turned on. The heroine crawls across the floor towards her Master, her leash dragging behind her. She has happily submitted to the god-like perfection that is Master Raffe. She is naked, like all his previous subs. He is dressed. She's been good and earned the privilege of time alone with her Master.

My brain is at war with my hormones as I read this. My brain says she's a simpering moron, but my hormones have me thinking I might want to sign up for that opportunity. It's been too long. Sam, the-one-night-stand, was my last sex time and that was six months ago. It was fast, drunk, and as clumsy as first-time sex always is.

The ringtone I have reserved for Carla pulls me back to reality. I was enjoying my alone time but she rarely calls me, so I pick up. She's not one to call just to chat.

"Viv?" She's crying. Actually, more like sobbing.

"Carla?" I only hear more sobbing. "Carla? What's wrong?" A chill crosses my entire body and instinctively I know something horrible has happened.

"He's gone."

I know she's referring to my dad.

"Gone? As in left you? Did you guys have a fight?" I grasp for the lesser of two disasters.

"No, baby, *gone*. Your dad had a heart attack this afternoon. He died, Viv. He died." She starts sobbing loudly again.

There is nothing I can say. I can't find any words. My throat is closing and I can't breathe. I continue holding the phone to my ear. I look around me at nothing, trying to grasp something that will tell me this isn't real, that I'm in some horrible dream and that I will wake up in a second.

Carla speaks again. "Oh God, Viv. This can't be real. He's too young."

I want to answer her but I still can't. The food in my stomach starts to churn and I think I might throw up.

"Viv? Are you there?"

Finally, a question I know the answer to. "Yeah, I'm here."

"Are you at home?"

I look around again, trying to remember exactly where I am. "No. I, um, I'm in Palm Springs for work." Now my brain has something to hold onto; planning, organizing. I suddenly know how to respond. The highly-ordered, always-prepared part of me says, "I'm going there, Carla. I'll get a flight out tonight. I'll be there in the morning."

"Okay."

"Do you have someone you can stay with tonight?" I go into mothering mode, taking care of Carla. It feels good; normal, settling.

"Yeah, I can call my friend Kate."

"Good, call Kate. Have her come get you. Take something so you can sleep. Okay?"

As always, the adult/child roles are reversed.

"Okay."

"Good. Call Kate now, have her stop and get you some sleep meds, and then I'll call you when I land tomorrow. Got it?"

"Yeah," she answers weakly. I hear her softening, relaxing a little as I take over.

"I'm going to hang up now. As soon as I do, you call Kate."

"I will." I'm about to hang up when she says, "Love you, Viv." It's a little odd. We've never been overly affectionate, but it feels fitting now.

"I love you too," I assure her and hang up.

I'm in full-on Vivienne mode in seconds, making a mental list of everyone I need to call and all I need to do: Book a ticket to New Orleans, talk to Bob, call Rach, call Danny... I'm going to have to put off that emotional punch in the gut for now. Will Danny even pick up the phone after our ugly fight so I can tell him his best friend has died? I can't believe I'm even worrying about our fight right now. It must be the shock talking.

My dad just died, for heaven's sake, and the only thing I feel is numb. My tear ducts are as dry as the Sahara.

CHAPTER 6

Fifteen hours later, I'm standing at the edge of the security zone watching for Danny to come through concourse B of the Louis Armstrong International Airport in New Orleans. My flight got in an hour and a half before his, so I told him I would rent a car and wait to give him a ride to the hotel. He seemed more lost than me when I reached out to him to break the news.

He must have been at work at the bar judging from the noise level in the background, and I was a little surprised he took my call. I played our conversation over and over in my head on the flight, analyzing if there would have been a better way or time to call. I also replayed all of my recent conversations with my dad, all of them painfully short and full of meaningless updates and banter.

I didn't cry as I packed in Palm Springs. I was too busy hammer-texting with Bob about the hotel and booking myself a flight. Bob offered to try to get one of the company jets for me, but I knew that would throw off not only the schedules of the execs but the pilots' too. I'm acutely aware of all the work that goes into getting a private jet from point A to point B. It's not like in the movies where the billionaire makes one call to command an immediate flight somewhere. I did, however, accept Bob's upgrade to first class on my commercial flight.

I didn't cry on the flight or after I landed, although being in the New Orleans airport and realizing I'm not going to see my dad hit me hard as I exited the gangway. I felt the pressure, the need to let something out; tears or a primal scream, but this was no place for either. After I claimed the car and got the keys, I lined up with all the happy families and loved ones waiting to greet someone coming home or coming to visit.

While watching a dad lift his son to get a drink from the water fountain, I realize... I'm an orphan. I have no parents. So many questions pop up in my mind that I never asked my dad—questions about him, questions about my mom. Questions I will never have an answer to now.

Danny approaches, but doesn't notice me. He doesn't seem to see much of anyone. He's just moving forward, one step at a time, looking towards nothing. I have to wait until he crosses the security line before I can touch his arm to get his attention. He half smiles at me.

"Vivey."

"Hey." I half smile back as I let the fact he called me Vivey again slide. There is something grounding about him being here as if part of my dad were with me now. Despite their age difference, their personalities were so much alike. I point towards the parking lot. "I got a car. I can go get it while you recover your bag and meet you out front."

He holds out the duffle he's carrying. "This is all I brought."

"Oh, okay. Well, let's get going." I lead the way toward the rental car lot.

The ride is uncomfortably silent; the voice of the app that's giving me driving directions is the only sound in the car. When we reach the hotel, I pull up in the drive and while I'm getting a valet ticket, Danny takes all our bags out of the trunk and stacks them so he can carry them all. I want to protest. I have a large suitcase, a hanging bag, a carry-on, and my briefcase tote since I was planning on being in Palm Springs for a week of semi-formal events. He lugs them inside without looking back at me.

Bob booked rooms for both Danny and me using his endless hotel points and coveted Black Membership status. He set us both up in concierge-level rooms at the JW Marriott down-town. At first, Danny protests and wants to pay, but I explain that it's all paid for by Bob's road warrior life.

"I'm going to Dad and Carla's in about an hour, then Carla and I have an appointment with Dad's lawyer. Do you want to go?" I want to establish our schedules before we part ways. Danny is following me to my room with all our bags. He doesn't seem interested in relinquishing the job to a valet, so I don't push the issue.

His voice is quieter than normal when he replies. "No."

"I'll call you when we're done and we can all go to dinner." It's a half request, half demand. I want him along for Carla and for me. I want to cling to the part of him that reminds me so much of my dad.

"Yeah, sure." He drops my bags inside my room and readjusts the duffle on his shoulder as he turns to leave.

I say, "Thank you" but I don't think he hears me over the loud noise of the door closing behind him.

I sit on edge of the bed, wondering what a normal person would do in this situation. I often wonder that. Would most people lie down on this giant pillow of a bed and sob? Would they raid the mini bar or call up for a bottle of liquor to drown their sorrows? All I want to do is organize. I don't want the noise of the TV or any distractions as I unpack and make the space my own. I light my soft rose-scented candle and arrange my toiletries in the bathroom. I lay out my travel pajamas and slippers for later. I hang my dresses and contemplate which one I should wear to the funeral and if any need pressing.

Oh, screw it. I love ironing and the way it quickly and efficiently makes perfection out of wrinkled chaos... I set up the ironing board and press all of them.

When I meet Carla at the lawyer's office, I see that she is my opposite. She isn't wearing make-up and her hair looks slept on. She looks the way someone grieving should look. I look like I'm attending a conference, complete with a notepad in a leather folder for taking notes during the meeting.

She hugs me tight and sobs and doesn't want to let go. It's only when her need for a Kleenex overwhelms her and she pulls away to wipe her nose on a tissue she pulls from the front pocket of her jeans. This would be an ideal time to fall apart, to break down while I've got someone here to commiserate my pain, but I can't seem to get there. I can't cry.

Carla thanked me at least ten times for being there during the meeting with the lawyer. My dad changed his will when he married Carla and split everything he had between us. I see relief when she hears the news. Before she married my dad, she was living on the edge of poverty. She got nothing from her first husband when they divorced after he went to jail. She has three sons by him, all of them grown, but they're more of a financial drain than a help to her. I'm not surprised that none of her children are here today, and I don't expect them at the funeral either.

I'm financially solid without my dad's money and I'm briefly tempted to just give it all to Carla, but I stop myself. If her kids leech off what she gets today, she might need it in the future.

After visiting with the lawyer, we stop by the funeral home Carla chose to make arrangements. My hackles are up and I'm not sure how to take the amount of upselling we're getting accompanied by a heaping dose of guilt.

I choose my words carefully. "I want this to represent my dad."

Carla nods and uses the water bottle she's carrying to splash her face with water. She starts to take out her cigarettes but realizes she probably can't smoke in here.

"Do you think Dad would want the premier line casket?"

She chuckles. "Heck, no. He'd go with a pine box if they'd let us."

I smile at how well she knows him. They'd only been married a few years but they were intensely happy, beautiful years for my dad. He and Carla were two peas in a pod.

"So we go with the basic package?"

She nods again.

"I'm not trying to be cheap," I assure her. "But you might need this money in the future more than we need some of this stuff now."

She gives me a solid nod. Like my dad, she's not much of a talker.

I was worried that dinner would be awkwardly quiet and just plain painful with three grieving people. It helped that Carla picked a hole-in-the-wall bar and grill where she and Dad liked to hang out. The regulars who knew my dad were game for a proper Irish wake with beer, whiskey, and stories all night.

Danny fit right in and had some of the best Big Mike stories since he was friends with him the longest. I shouldn't have been, but I was shocked at some of the scrapes Danny and Dad had with the law.

"Big Mike and I had some great times together, but the time we spent fixing up that old car of his were some of the best. We spent more time fussing over that old Goat than all the other cars we'd ever owned combined. But she is a beaut. There was many a night Carla would catch us out in the garage tinkering under the hood, well beyond midnight," Danny said.

"What kinda car was it?" the bartender asks, setting another beer on the bar.

"A 1965 Pontiac GTO, or 'The Goat,' as we called it. Boy oh boy, did Big Mike and I have a blast taking it for test spins through the marshlands outside Savannah. Once we got that baby up and running, we had to talk our way out of a few speeding tickets," Danny chuckles. "We even tried to outrun the cops one time, dying to see how fast the old Goat would go. But as hard as we tried, there was no wiggling our way out of that ticket. Big Mike tried though, he even offered to let the cop take The Goat for a spin." Danny raises his glass into the air. "To The Goat. And the best friend I've ever had, Mike Ramsey."

"To Big Mike!" everyone hollers, splashing their beer and whiskey as they bang their glasses together.

I laugh until I cry at the stories but still can't let go and grieve. Lack of sleep and too much whiskey overtake me around midnight but none of us is in any shape to drive. I impress the hell out of all the old dudes in the bar when I order an Uber using my phone and explain how I have an account and don't require cash to pay. This brings on rounds of stories of how proud my dad was of me and how he would tell anyone who would listen about his smart, beautiful daughter. I almost lose it, but the car arrives and saves me from becoming a blubbering mess.

The Uber driver drops Carla at home before driving Danny and me back to our hotel. In the elevator on the way up to our rooms, Danny watches me. I'm not sure whether he's waiting for me to fall over and burst into tears or if he's analyzing my lack of tears. He doesn't explain. He scooches closer to me until our shoulders are touching and as he gently moves his fingers back and forth, they feel like feathers brushing up against the back of my hand. As the elevator opens, I take a step forward and he reaches for my hand, giving it a squeeze.

It's not like Danny to show me affection. It's not something I expected. I want so much to hug him but I can't even look at him. Instead, as I pull away, I whisper, "Night, Danny," and head straight for my room.

CHAPTER 7

My dad was a big man in physique and in personality. I am doubtful his funeral will do him justice. It's being held at a small church, one of Carla's choosing. She and my dad had recently attended a friend's wedding here. She told me she'd fallen in love with the dark wooden beams and charming stained glass windows.

As I step inside, I see why she loves it. It is simple, warm and welcoming, with row after row of traditional wooden pews. The stained glass windows are stunningly beautiful and the sunlight beaming through them is casting a kaleidoscope of colours onto the pews. As I make my way to the front of the church, the fragrant aroma of fresh flowers welcomes me.

There are so many bouquets. Beside Carla's sits the one I ordered with the large white sash which reads "DAD" across the front. Two dozen pure white roses, deep green leaves, some wooden accents, and baby's breath mixed in. It looks rustic and soft, like my dad; rough around the edges but soft as a marshmallow on the inside. It's perfect.

I'm glad Carla decided on a closed casket. If it was open and

I could see my dad lying there, I'm not sure I could get through this without losing it completely. The casket is draped with his favourite dark brown throw—the one he would use when he sat by the fireplace on cool evenings. On top sits a framed eight-by-ten-inch photo of my dad taken shortly after he and Carla were married. It's one of the few photos where his grin is so big his whole face is lit up. Apparently, it was taken on an evening when he'd had a bit too much to drink and was feeling more jovial than usual. My dad had such a great laugh. I can't believe I'll never hear it again.

We don't expect many people at the funeral; a few from the bar, the man Dad worked for and his family, and some of Carla's coworkers. As people arrive, I realize how few of them I know. It's strange to be at my own dad's funeral and meeting many of the other mourners for the first time. I feel like an outsider and I wonder if it's my own fault. I wanted my independence. I pushed him away. Am I paying the price now?

Most of the guys he worked with in Savannah, the friends I know, can't make it on such short notice. They've sent flowers and donations in Dad's name to his favourite charities. Some even left heartfelt messages on the church's funeral webpage. Their long-distance love helps me feel a little less disconnected.

Danny stays on the periphery of the event. He's a quiet man who looks incredibly handsome but uncomfortable in his suit and tie, just like my dad. Not being an actual part of the family he has no role, no script to follow like I do to pass these sad hours. I want to go to him, to stand by him and hold his hand, but every time I try, someone else vies for my attention.

At two p.m., the funeral director gathers all those present for a brief memorial service. Carla asked me to speak, but I struggled with something to say as I lay in bed last night and the perfect speech eluded me. To do justice to the loving but frustrating and complicated relationship we had, I would need to speak for hours. Even then, I'm not sure I could get it right. When my mom died, we became a family of two, but two never felt like a family. It felt more like a couple of people who lived together and crossed paths and sometimes butted heads. We cared for each other and took care of each other, but my mom's absence was like a missing puzzle piece that had tied us together. Big Mike Ramsey, all-American tough guy, did the best he could raising a daughter alone.

I was happy for him when he met Carla and decided to move to New Orleans for her. He had been single for fifteen years, although I learned last night, hardly celibate. There were days I missed him, but I was mostly happy he had moved on and found love again. I was also happy to have him out of my hair. It hurts to even think that now. But at the time, I was ready to make my own life and stop taking care of him and having him jump into my life at the most inopportune times.

There is no way to express how I feel about my dad in a few minutes to a group of people I hardly know, so I let the funeral director say a few generic things—a choice I will likely regret later.

After the service finishes, Danny and I accompany Carla to the cemetery. During the ten-minute drive, none of us speaks a word. As we exit the car, the earthy smell of fresh-mowed grass mixed with a hint of moss hits my nostrils. There are highly polished tombstones with deep etchings and others so old and worn the writing on them is illegible.

"My grandparents four generations back are buried in this cemetery," says Carla.

I nod and continue to take it all in. There are a few groups gathered in the distance, too far away for me to hear anything, but I imagine they are saying their final goodbyes to a loved one. The clouds above threaten rain, something I've prepared for by bringing along an oversized umbrella.

We make our way to a corner of the cemetery, quite a way from the road to where my dad's plot is. The graves immediately around his are well maintained, many with fresh flowers either planted or placed in front of them. There is a giant oak tree close by. Its branches stretch wide enough that even on the sunniest of days, Dad will always remain in the shade. The tree seems to be a favoured perch; while I can't see them, I can hear the sweet sounds of the birds overhead. Their chirps are almost rhythmic as if they are having a conversation, letting each other know there is a new arrival below. It's a welcome sound of life in what is otherwise a sober and quiet place.

There is only the three of us standing in silence as the casket lowers into the ground. There should be thousands; all the people he helped, mentored and loved. This is some sick twist of fate—that he died suddenly and far from home. To keep myself from facing the stark reality of this moment, I focus instead on all the things I might have done to make it better. Should I specifically have asked more people to drive to the cemetery for the burial? Would more of his Savannah friends be here if I had contacted them sooner?

The funeral director says a final few words. Carla's eyes are fixed ahead, her cheeks stained black from running mascara. The wad of Kleenex in her hand is reduced to mush. I put one arm around her as I search in my purse for fresh tissues. I feel Danny's warm presence to my left and for a moment and I let myself wish I had someone, meaning him, to hold me up. My super powers are wavering right now as I rely on my umbrella to steady me.

I console myself with the truth that I've never had a shoulder to cry on, and it would probably feel kind of odd and uncomfortable. Growing up, my dad never knew what to do when I cried. He might pat me on the back and offer a few encouraging words but never a warm embrace. Female tears scared him. I'm better at being the shoulder that others cry on. I may not always know what to say, but I'm fantastic at knowing what to do. I focus on Carla, holding her more tightly and rubbing her back.

The funeral director concludes by asking Carla if she would like to say anything. She gently shakes her head from side to side as she takes hold of my hand and gives it a squeeze. My voice quivers as I whisper the words, "I love you, Dad" and toss a single white rose onto his casket. Carla forces a weak smile and motions for us to leave.

Danny and I pick up take-out for dinner and take it back to Carla and Dad's place. Although I could use a good dose of cooking therapy right now, I don't want to invade Carla's kitchen. I have to let procuring the perfect restaurant meals suffice for tonight.

Carla's touched I remember her and Dad's favourite Chinese restaurant and her standard order: shrimp lo mien, no mushrooms. It makes me happy because not everyone understands how I love; by paying attention, by remembering their likes and the things that matter to them.

We eat in relative silence in the dining room as I look around and notice the photos of my Dad on top of the china cabinet. Peering out towards the living room, I spot Dad's Savannah Banana baseball cap laying on the back of his favourite chair. He may have moved to New Orleans, but he remained faithful to his hometown baseball team. On one of the living room walls, the little model cars he enjoyed building are prominently displayed. I can't help but feel we are in for a long night ahead until Carla speaks up.

"It's Wednesday night." She clears her throat, striving to sound upbeat. "Your dad and I always watch *Survivor* on Wednesdays. Would you want to stay and watch it with me?"

I love the idea of my dad and Carla and all their rituals; the little things that bound them together. Those were the things that made me feel like I was part of a family when I visited them —Sunday afternoon football games, dinner and a movie every Friday night, Wednesdays watching *Survivor*. Continuing the pattern feels good.

"Sounds good. I haven't seen this season," I say, trying to keep the mood light.

"You two go and get it started and I'll bring some dessert into the other room." Bowls of ice cream eaten in front of the TV were also part of every Wednesday night.

I stand, start to clear plates and close take-out box lids, but Carla stops me. "Let me. You've done so much already. Go, get out of those heels and get comfortable. I'll join you in a few minutes."

She needs to have a job, a task to keep her in motion and preoccupied. I go to the bathroom to gather myself and make sure I don't have mascara pools under my eyes.

When I walk into the living room, Danny is sitting where I normally sit on the couch. He has unbuttoned his dress shirt about a third of the way down to compensate for the way Carla keeps the house barely air conditioned. It's embarrassing how much it affects me, even today. My lust for him has no bounds, no conscience, and obviously no scruples.

I figure I better play it safe and not sit on the couch with him. Carla's chair and Dad's recliner surround a small end table on the other side of the room. I decide to take Dad's lumpy, old recliner but stop before I can cross the room. My heart lurches. I've been sucker-punched in the gut. The stupid chair is my undoing.

My dad and I had a horrible, electrifying argument when I was seventeen and going through an HGTV/DIY phase of redecorating. I had a plan for our living room and wanted my dad's ugly recliner gone. There was no place for it in my design scheme. As I look at it now, I hear all the ugly things I said to him about cheap-ass furniture and him being stubborn and unreasonable. I even called him a jackass that evening.

I'm stuck. I can't move. I'm silently crying when I hear Danny call my name. "Vivey?" I don't answer; I can't seem to get out of this sad place. I'm in deep, trying to wish my dad back so I can apologize. I need more time with him.

Danny stands next to me, and I know this because I hear him say, "Vivey" in my ear.

The ball of emotion caught in my chest since Palm Springs rises and I can't stop it. I double over and gasp for breath. Danny rubs my back, unsure what to do for me. I collapse on to him as my need for comfort overwhelms me. He pulls me down with him onto the couch and holds me close.

And I sob.

Tears pour out of me and the harder I cry, the closer he holds me—until it's almost hard to breathe with his strong arms compressing me. I'm falling apart and he tries to hold me together.

"He's gone," I choke out, then hiccup as I try to breathe in.

Danny smooths my hair with one hand while the other keeps me pinned to his shoulder. I feel him breathing unevenly, fighting his own pain and tension.

"I want him back," I wail. "I want him back."

"I know." His voice cracks and one of his tears slides from his face and onto mine.

Flinging my arm over his other shoulder, I turn my face into his neck and hold him tight. I force in a breath past the hiccups. Danny smells like woody cologne with the underlying scent of jet fuel, the scent that always clung to my dad's skin too.

When I finally calm myself enough to stop crying, I'm spent. I don't know when I've ever felt this exhausted. I struggle to lift my head from Danny's shoulder, but he pushes me back down and gently kisses my forehead. I muster enough strength to squeeze his shoulder and lean in to kiss his neck. It feels so natural, kissing him, probably because I've conjured it so many times in my mind. I do it again and feel a rush of endorphins wash through my tired brain. I turn my head to kiss his jaw. His whiskers feel exactly like I knew they would against my lips: sensual, rough.

I must have shocked him. He turns his head toward me and there they are, those bewitching kissable lips. It's more instinctual than planned when I lean up and gently kiss them. They feel just as good as I knew they would. I kiss him again and I'm blindsided by a wave of desire. I want more. I want to kiss his warm lips for hours. I want to feel them all over my body, everywhere I hurt, kissing away all my pain and weariness.

Just as a little voice starts to remind me that Danny doesn't want this, that he doesn't want me, his arms pull me closer. He kisses me back—and I shove that little voice away and let myself fall into this beautiful floating feeling. I'm tipsy, almost drunk; definitely out of my head, for once. I'm only vaguely aware of Carla coming into the room. Danny breaks the kiss and we pull apart, but not before she sees us.

She chuckles and shakes her head. "He always wondered when you two would get together."

Her words stun both Danny and me, and we turn and look at her in unison.

"He would talk to you on the phone." She gestures to Danny with the bowl of ice cream she's carrying. "Then after he would hang up, he would always say that one of these days you were going to pull your head out of your ass and finally grab onto Vivey."

Danny is too stunned to speak. All I can do is laugh at the irony and appreciate the way Carla quoted my dad perfectly.

He turns to me. "Did you?"

"Know?" I shake my head. "He never said anything to me." But it would have been nice, Dad. There was too much left unsaid.

Carla hands us each a bowl of ice cream. "Rocky Road," she says, smiling like a Cheshire cat. She un-pauses *Survivor* and sits down with her own bowl.

I eat my ice cream and try to focus on the show, but I can't stop looking at Danny. He looks like he is going over every conversation he ever had with my dad about me. He's so lost in his thoughts his ice cream melts before he ever takes a spoonful.

We finish watching *Survivor* with Carla, linger on our goodbyes, and promise we will come by tomorrow before we fly home. I know she's spent nights here without Dad before, but it's still hard to leave her alone.

Danny remains quiet on the car ride to the hotel. I catch him looking over at me occasionally.

"What?" I ask.

He shrugs.

"Talk to me." I want to reach for his hand, but I'm not sure where his head is right now.

"Do you remember when you moved into your apartment?"

My dad, Danny, Rach, and Luis all helped me move in, but only Danny stuck around to put the bed together. Everyone else had somewhere to be that night. It was yet another occasion when I pretty much threw myself at him and he shut me down. "Yeah, I remember."

He watches the road, lost in thought. "I wanted to stay."

What? My mouth is open but I can't speak. He wanted to stay!

"It was about two months after she left." He never says his

ex-wife's name. "I told myself I was rebounding, that your Dad would kill me, that you'd regret it. But I wanted to stay."

"But you never... I didn't think you liked me. I mean, I thought you were only nice to me because of Dad."

"I've gone out of my way, more than once, to drive by your place." He chuckles to himself, finally turning to me. "I've thought about stopping in, pretending to check up on you, just to hang out with you for a while."

"Why didn't you?"

He shrugs, goes back to watching the road, and then replies, "It wouldn't have been a good idea, even if I didn't believe Mike would kill me. I was usually feeling sorry for myself."

"But I would have—"

He doesn't let me finish. "Not fair to you."

And there it is again: He and my Dad, thinking for me, telling me what I want and need, never asking my opinion. "Don't you think that's for me to decide? I know how to take care of myself, Danny."

By looking over at me, he stresses his sincerity. "I know you do."

He's quiet the rest of the way to the hotel, but when we get there he touches me more than he has since I've known him. He offers his hand to help me out of the car and holds mine in the elevator. He must be still torn about us, since he's studying the carpet. He finally looks at me when we hear the chime announcing we've reached our floor.

When the door opens, he lets go of my hand and steps off. I follow and stand waiting to see if he will tell me what he's been thinking.

"I'm not going to tell you what to do." He glares at me. "But I am going to lay it all out there." Taking my hand, he studies our entwined fingers. "I'm too old for you. I'm broke. I have a bitch of an ex-wife." I know all these things, so he brushes through them. But he studies my reaction when he says, "And I'm leaving."

My heart jolts at the last word. "You're leaving? What do you mean you're leaving? Where are you going?"

"I've taken a job in Saudi Arabia. I leave in two months." He softly brushes the hair from my face. "This is a bad time to tell you. I'm sorry. I want you to know before we..." He leaves a blank space for what might happen between us.

"Why?" I ask, while pretty much knowing why. There's always a need for airplane mechanics in Saudi and it pays a shit ton, tax free. Guys go there to make money—a lot of it.

"Remember when Nick was born, he had that heart thing?"

I nod. Danny's son was born premature and had a heart defect, but he had several surgeries when he was little to fix it. Or so I thought.

"Well, there's been complications. He's doing okay now, but he's on some new experimental drug and treatment. It's not covered by insurance."

"Oh, wow." I shake my head. "I had no idea."

"I've signed a three-year contract."

I nod and exhale my frustration. It feels like a cruel joke. After ten years, I find out that he wants me, and he's leaving. We're both emotionally wrung out from the funeral, and now this.

He leans in and rests his forehead against mine. "I'm sorry." Wrapping his other hand around my waist, he pulls me in for a hug.

I say, "I'm sorry too" into his collar.

"What are you sorry for?" he asks.

"For me. For you. For us." I sigh and burrow farther into his warm neck. "For Carla, for Dad." My voice cracks, and he pulls me close with both arms. "Come sleep with me." I sense him start to pull away and add, "I mean sleep, as in go to sleep. Don't let me lie there alone in my room and overthink all this."

"How can I stop that?"

"If you're sleeping next to me, possibly without this annoying shirt," I bump his collar with my nose, "I won't think about much of anything else."

He laughs softly and kisses my forehead. "All right. We'll just sleep." I can tell he's as tired as I am, but there's still a question in his voice whether that's all we'll do.

In my room, standing on opposite sides of the bed, we strip. I catch him slowly scan me up and down, making me feel excited and vulnerable at the same time. He takes off his socks and shoes, jacket and shirt, but leaves his dress pants on. We lock eyes as I unbuckle my shoes and toss them on the floor and pull my dress over my head. I stop, momentarily trying to remember which bra and undies I have on. I look down. It's my pink lace set, more sweet than sexy, but it makes me feel pretty when I'm sad. Danny raises his eyebrows at it and smiles. I pull back the covers and slide into bed. Danny's still standing there.

"That's what you're wearing to sleep?" I nod and pull back the covers on his side. He shakes his head in protest but slides in between the sheets, still wearing his pants, and turns off the lamp before settling on the pillow. I scoot across until my head is on his chest and my leg wrapped around his.

"I'm supposed to sleep like this?" he asks. His hand caresses my back.

I relax into him. "For now."

"You're not making this easy."

"I don't want to" is my drowsy reply. I don't torture him anymore, but only because I drift off immediately.

I'm awake before the sun and for a half-hour I lie here watching Danny sleep as I try not to move and wake him. I don't care if it's only for a short time. When he told me he was leaving last night, I was crushed; so crushed I had to push the information aside and forget about it so I could get some sleep.

When I woke up this morning, I knew exactly what I wanted to do. I want to be with Danny for as long as I can.

I've been thinking about my dad and Carla. Would they have missed the chance to be so in love if they had known it would end so soon? Heck, no. I'm glad Dad quit his job to move to New Orleans and be with Carla. I'm glad he had those few years when he wasn't lonely anymore. His life is giving me my answer.

I reach for Danny's hand and interlace my fingers with his. He mumbles something and rolls away from me, taking my hand with him. I'm now squished up against his back, so I take advantage of it.

I touch my cheek to his warm skin and breathe in. I'm imprinting his smell on my brain because it makes me so damn happy. He twitches and mumbles again, then rolls onto his back and slowly opens his eyes. With my chin on his chest, I look up at him and smile.

"Morning."

He doesn't respond, and I get the feeling he isn't a morning person. Still, he moves his arm from under me up around my shoulder and pulls me in close. We lie here in silence, but I can only stay quiet for so long.

"I thought about what you said last night, and I don't care if we can only be together for a short time. Do you think my dad would have stayed away from Carla if he had known it would only be for a few years?"

With my head against his shoulder, I can't see his face but hear him take a deep breath. He rubs my arm for a few minutes before he says, "No."

"I get why you're leaving. I don't like that you are, but I get it."

I take my hand from his and rub it up his arm. He has a faded farmer's tan on his bicep where his uniform shirt ends. I've noticed it before and wanted to touch him there. So I do.

"Let's do this—for right now, for the time we've got," I tell him.

I caress his forearm, the muscles and tendons I've watched bunch and flex as he worked with my dad. I want to touch him everywhere and I'm getting turned on, but I'm not feeling much movement from him. I pull away to look at his face.

He's debating again.

"What?" I ask.

"I should warn you, it's been almost two years." He shakes his head and laughs. "Two long years." He looks at me. "I don't want this to be bad, but..."

I don't understand. I would expect after two years of no sex he would be on me like white on rice. I want to roll on top of him and get this party started, so I move and he eases me off.

"Vivey, do you know what happens when a man hasn't had sex in two years?" I have to admit I don't. "I'm gonna be like a goddamn teenager again. You are killing me right now."

He might have been trying to warn me off by telling me that he was going to be bad in bed, but all I heard was that I was killing him. Me. I feel like a goddess who can turn on this beautiful man.

I know my smile is wicked, but I can't help it. I'm having too much fun. *Drive you crazy and kill you with sex? Challenge accepted.* I lean down and kiss his chest, then his belly button. I want to pleasure him.

"God damn, Vivey." I can hear his conflict: *Stop, but...don't.* "Come here," he says pulling me close. "Are you sure this is what you want?"

"Absolutely," I say tugging at his dress pants.

CHAPTER 9

It seems I was a little premature, feeling smug and thinking I had a few things to show Danny. Round One took the edge off him, helping to relieve his two year build-up of sexual tension. And it made Round Two an eye-opening lesson for me.

I thought I'd had pretty good sex in the past. I mean, it was fun and felt... good. But it was all fast-food sex; quick, served a purpose, just the basics. I thought that was all there was until Danny introduced me to gourmet sex.

Sure, I had always assumed he'd be good in bed because one, who fantasizes about crappy sex? And two, there's something in his walk, an ease in his body that says he's uninhibited and confident. I got that part right. But, I didn't know that was just the tip of the iceberg. What I got this morning is a fantastic lover—something I thought only existed in steamy romance novels.

After Round One, he's in no hurry to go again, whereas I'm definitely ready. I try to move things along, reaching for him. But he takes my hand, interlocking our fingers. Then he places my hands over my head and half rolls onto me. I'm trapped in the best way, at the mercy of his pace.

He leans in and nudges the tender skin on my neck with his lips and stubble. It sets off a ripple of sensations through my body and my hips begin to wiggle.

"Slow down," he whispers to me.

My knee-jerk reaction is to do the opposite. I hate it when someone tells me what to do. But I realize he's right. I've wanted this, exactly what's happening right this minute, for years. I've dreamed about it, and now I'm going to rush through it?

I stop fighting him, pushing against him, and relax under his weight. It feels so good.

"That's it." He tries to encourage me, but all I hear is a patronizing tone. I'm having a hard time letting go of the fight we've been having for the past two years, and I tense up again. He notices.

"What's wrong?"

"What's wrong?" What's wrong is that I'm me—uptight, neurotic, overbearing me.

"Vivey, relax."

Nerves and frustration bubble up into a laugh. "Me, relax? When have you ever seen me relaxed?"

He knows me well enough to chuckle at the idea. "I haven't. But I want to."

Danny has ignited nerves all the way to my toes; every inch of my body wants him. He excites parts of me I'd never thought about during sex. The front of my thighs feel the hair on his legs and the muscles beneath. My belly feels soft against his and my breasts are tickled by the hair on his chest. He's moved from kissing my neck to my shoulders and then my clavicle. I doubt most guys would know where my clavicle is, let alone how kissing me there would fire so many sensitive nerves.

I can feel his skin getting warmer. Still, he's in no hurry. He's meticulously making his way down my body, blissfully torturing me. My urge to take over and get relief is over-whelming.

I try rubbing my hip against him but he pulls away, denying me access. I scoot closer, but he sets his strong lower leg over my hips to keep me in place. What the hell is wrong with me? I'm turning lovemaking with the man of my dreams into a WWE grudge match.

I can't begin to hide my tension. He stops kissing me, and lets go of my hands. "I'm sorry," I whisper.

Rolling me onto my side, he spoons me from behind. "It's all right. First times together are never easy." We lie here for a minute, and I worry that he's giving up on me.

"Don't stop, please," I say, and immediately regret it. Wow, now I'm begging. *Please have sex with the insane control freak.*

I feel his lips smile against my shoulder. "I haven't. I'm still holding you." But he pulls away and I panic. I've pushed him too far.

He tells me to stay right there as he gets out of bed. I'm so relieved he'll be back that I ignore the fact he just gave me a command. I roll over to watch him. He finds his wallet and digs deep into the lining before producing a smashed, battered condom package. He flips it around in his hand.

"Do these expire?"

I laugh and relax and fall more in love with him—the wonderful laid-back sexy man who can stand there naked and make jokes. I hop out of bed and dash into the bathroom for my toiletries bag and my own supply of condoms. I toss five fresh condoms on the bed and Danny raises one eyebrow at me. I'm not sure if he's impressed I'm prepared or worried I carry a supply with me.

"What?"

He picks them up. "Five?"

I laugh. "I can get more if we need them."

Danny opens one and slides it on as I watch. His openness

with his body makes me less concerned about mine. I take off my bra and toss it across the room and slingshot my panties in his direction. I miss by a mile, but I'm having so much fun.

"We'll do this your way, this time." He pulls me in for a kiss. "But you will let me have my way with you eventually. We have two months to figure this out."

I get out of my head and just feel, and our sex moves into an entirely new realm—a dance of give and take. And I feel it like I never have before. The heat of our bodies as they melt together and slide apart is exhilarating. I'm immersed in the moment, not lost in my own head worried about my performance, his name escapes my quivering lips and I fall back. An euphoric, spent pile of mush, and I laugh at absolutely nothing, my entire body still trembling. Danny catches his breath and smiles. I don't know what to say. What I feel is beyond words. Luckily, he doesn't seem to be looking for conversation either.

When I finally do get the energy to speak, all I can say is, "Wow."

He lazily rubs his hand along my arm. "Wow?"

He's questioning this? Did he not just have mind-blowing sex with me? Or is he questioning whether he was that good?

It dawns on me then that he hasn't used his substantial skills on a woman in a long time, let alone an appreciative woman. I lean up and kiss him on his chest.

"Yeah," I assure him. "Wow."

CHAPTER 10

Danny and I arrive back at Dad and Carla's house, and I notice the morning newspaper on the lawn. As I bend down to retrieve it I think of how my dad's day always started with the paper and a coffee. Today, a wonderful light breeze makes the leaves appear to dance on their branches. I close my eyes for a moment and turn my head towards the sun, soaking up its warmth on my face. I can't help but wonder if my dad's out there somewhere, looking down on us. It's oddly comforting to me, believing he is.

We spend the morning at Carla's house, delaying our inevitable departure and her being completely alone. She digs through drawers and papers, offering me stuff I might want or need. In Dad's top dresser drawer she finds pictures of me as a kid and a few of my dad and mom together. I'm grateful to have those and immediately put them in my purse.

"What about The Goat?" she asks when she comes across the keys to the car Danny and my dad had fixed up.

I answer her but look at Danny. "What about The Goat? It's more his than mine."

"It's yours." She hands me the keys. "I've already got a car, and I can't drive that thing."

Danny's eyes are on the keys. I can see he wants it and all he has now is his motorcycle. He did half the work on it, and it's his tie to my dad. I hold the keys out to him but he shakes his head. "It's yours. He left it to you."

"But…"

"I can't take it with me anyway."

I had forgotten about his job in Saudi or pushed it out of my mind on purpose.

Carla sees another opportunity to keep us with her for a little while longer. "Well, let's go see if the darn thing even starts. It's been months since he drove it."

I hand Danny the keys. It can be finicky when you start it and he'll know how to finesse and coax it. I know this because Rach and I have borrowed the car a few times through the years. But, this isn't the time to share that.

The moment it turns over and roars to life, we are all still and silent. It's like my dad is here. The loud sound, the oversized energy, the precision of the mechanics are all Big Mike's signature in this world. I do want the car and I want Danny to have it too. We both need this piece of my dad.

We drive around a few blocks, letting the battery charge, silently enjoying the feeling of my dad's presence. When we get back to the house, none of us want to get out of the car. As we sit in the driveway, I know exactly what I need to do.

"I'm driving this home."

"Today?" Carla questions.

"Yeah." I nod my head, picturing the perfection of the idea. Then my perfect idea grows, fate giving me a push that Danny and I should have more time together. "You coming with me?" I challenge him.

He doesn't answer right away, but I know he can't resist

driving Dad's baby back to Savannah. He looks around the interior, assessing the odds of the car making it six hundred and fifty miles. "Yeah, I can't let you drive this thing home alone. I'm not sure it'll make it."

And he's back to treating me like a child. I smirk at him. "And what are you going to do if it doesn't?"

He smirks back. "I'm the mechanic who built it. I'm sure I can think of something. What do you think you would do alone?"

I lift my phone and point to the AAA app. "They have tools; you don't."

Carla laughs at us from the back seat. "I wish I could be there to see the two of you on this road trip."

I smile back at her and point to my texting app. "I'll send you updates."

After turning in the rental car and canceling our flights, we go to a huge truck stop on the edge of the city for provisions. It's near seven p.m. and the sun is setting.

"Why don't I drive to Mobile while you sleep, and then we can decide whether to take I-10 through Florida or go through Alabama?" As I talk, I follow Danny through the store, both of us gathering snacks.

"One, you aren't driving, I am; and two, we are not going through Florida." He pours himself a large black coffee and I hand him two sugar packets. "Two?" he wonders, as if I'd forgotten his preference.

"It's a large," I note, pointing at the thirty-two-ounce coffee cup. He doesn't reply but dumps both packets into his cup. "My map app shows six construction zones on the Alabama route. It might be forty miles longer though Florida, but it will be much faster and easier to drive."

He silently studies the map on my phone before reluctantly giving in. "Fine, Florida."

"And there is no reason for you to drive the entire way. I'm more than capable."

"Vivey, you can't handle that car. It's fast; the steering has too much give—"

"And the brake pedal sticks," I finish his sentence. "I know, I have driven it many times." I let him process that bombshell while I peruse the selection of granola bars.

"Big Mike let you drive that car?"

"Rach and I borrowed it a couple of times, and I'm pretty sure my dad didn't know about it." I grab two protein bars to go with my iced tea.

"You stole the car."

The way he says it irritates me to no end—so damn patronizing. We've started something new, but it's not going to be easy to let go of what we've been to each other these past few years.

I don't reply to his accusation because I want to tell him where to stick it and not in a sexy way. Instead, I walk toward the register and ask if he wants an apple or banana from the fruit basket as we pass it.

He refuses to sleep, but lets me drive the first leg of the trip to Mobile, saying he wants proof I know how to drive it. I keep it just above the speed limit and obey all the traffic laws, even though I'm itching to push it. Driving the car brings back great memories of flying down long, low marshland roads with the windows down and the stereo turned up. I laugh to myself at the memory of Rach throwing herself at the cop who stopped us. At eighteen, she was more silly than sexy—and in the end, I'm sure the cop let us off with a warning because he was impressed with the car, not us.

When I let Danny take over on the far side of Mobile, he visibly relaxes, like he'd held his breath the entire time I was driving. He eases back into the seat, lets his hand drape across the steering wheel and gear shift, and tunes into the powerful hum of the engine. God, he's sexy—in his element.

The sun has set and the night air is cool in the quiet, sparsely populated Florida panhandle. I want to talk to him, not sleep. I want to find the kind, attentive man I fell in love with. The one who existed before my dad left and assigned him the job of my keeper. The one who had an open heart before his wife left him.

The magic of the moment works and our conversation flows easily. We start to fall back into the friendship we had when I was younger. He opens up about his son and his heart relapse, the experimental drugs he's taking and the costs.

"One injection, one damn shot, was over two grand. And he had to get the shot for six months in a row." He shakes his head in frustration. "That put me behind, and then he had a reaction to the shots and was in the hospital for a few weeks—scared the shit out of me. That was partially covered, but I sold my car to cover the deductibles."

I try to just listen and let him vent, to offer some comfort. I don't think he's had anyone to share all this with since my dad left. But I can't just listen. I'm programmed to fix. If someone presents me with a problem, I need to find a solution. That's just how I'm programmed. And like the pieces of a puzzle falling into place, I see it. I know I can help Danny get back on his feet faster and give us some time together. The problem is that the guy who sees it as his job to take care of me will probably be less than enthusiastic about my idea.

"Hell, no!"

Yeah, that's pretty much what I figured he would say. He's insulted, so I need to lay out all the reasons why my idea is flawless.

"If you move out of your house now, it will be easier to sell and take care of before you leave. I can help you get rid of stuff and put things in storage. In fact, I'm gonna need a storage garage for this car. We can get a more sizable one, split it, and you can store your stuff in there while you're gone."

He doesn't respond right away, which means he's mulling it

over. He takes so long to reply that I think he's not going to; finally, he says, "I can't mooch off you." I should be thrilled because it sounds like he might be willing, but his harsh view of himself and the situation stops me short.

"Danny, moving in with me is not…"

I start to give him my logical perspective, we're friends helping each other out, but I realize that there is no room for reason here. It's killing me to see him hurting and to know I have a solution. If he would only see it from my point of view…

Although I drop the subject, it still sits heavy between us. I wish I hadn't said it. I didn't mean to kick this good man when he was already down. We have nothing to say to each other for the next few hours.

The sun is coming up and Danny looks exhausted. I check the hotel app on my phone.

"There's a Fairfield coming up in Jacksonville. They have free breakfast and we could eat and sleep for a few hours."

My helpfulness seems to irritate him more. "I'm not going to let you pay for a hotel room. I'll get some coffee and we'll keep going."

I would let him be right, for once, if his plan wasn't so dangerous. He needs sleep to keep driving and it doesn't look like his crushed male ego is going to let me take over any time soon.

"I'm not paying for it," I say, and remind him, "points."

"Bob's points?"

"Technically, yes, but they're also my points to use. He never uses them. When he's not traveling for work, he doesn't like to go anywhere."

Danny briefly considers it and then shakes his head. I switch tactics.

"I'm tired, Danny, and hungry. I'd like to take a shower and change clothes." I hate resorting to a take-care-of-me plea, but we need to stop and it's a way to put him in charge. I add, "Please."

"Fine. Tell me how to get there," he says on a resigned breath, then mumbles, "Like there's a chance you won't."

We eat breakfast in silence, focusing on the news playing on the flat screen at the far end of the room—our silent stalemate a painful reminder of how much I've already screwed things up.

In our room, I shower first. When I finish, he's sound asleep on one of the two double beds, wearing only his briefs. I stand and watch him, his large, beautiful male body sprawled across the bed. I'm getting chilled; my hair is still wet and I'm wearing only a towel in the air-conditioned room.

I want him. I want his warmth. I want his affection; his arms around me, his heart beating close to my ear. I think about taking the other bed and leaving him alone, but I remember Dad and Carla and their short time together. Seize the moment, girl. I peel off the towel, lay it on the pillow and slide into the small space next to him. He wakes and looks at me. I look back, pleading with my eyes, completely vulnerable, raw and naked— risking a very painful rejection. He gives in, huffing out a frustrated sigh before he pulls me close and spoons me. This is not the way I had pictured things between us, not what I had hoped for.

When I awake, the afternoon sun is seeping through the cracks in the drapes. I'm facing him and he's breathing deeply. I reach out to caress him and hesitantly touch one of his nipples, wondering if that feels as good to him as it does to me. He stirs briefly and smiles in his sleep. Interesting.

My eyes slowly trace his face as if I must capture it to memory. I reach up and glide my hand ever so gently along the side of his face following the curve of his jawline. He's still half asleep, but I'm enjoying this time with him. Lying here feeling his warmth, mesmerized by the rise and fall of his chest, I scooch a little closer and continue to explore his body with my hands. This gets his attention. He opens his eyes and smiles lazily at me.

"I could get used to being woken up this way." I like the way he says it, like he's warming up to the idea of us living together.

"I could get used to waking you up this way." I smile back. I feel close to him at this moment, connected like a real couple.

CHAPTER 11

As we reach the outskirts of Savannah, the sun is setting and I plot the logistics of Danny and I staying together tonight. Unfortunately, I don't see any way for it to happen, especially when we both have to go to work tomorrow. I reluctantly ask him to drop me at my place so he can take the car to his house.

We block all the parking spaces behind my building as we unload my suitcases. I take my carry-on bag and Danny grabs the rest. As we are going up the back steps, my neighbor, Mrs. Ogden, opens her door.

"Vivienne, I thought that was you." She looks at me briefly and then studies Danny. "I haven't seen you around much lately."

"No, I've been out of town. Were you looking for me? Can I help you with something?"

"Oh no, I'm fine, but I took a delivery for you." She seems a little irritated, which is odd. We accept packages for each other all the time.

"Oh, okay. Well, I can take it now if you'd like."

She slips inside her door and returns hid behind the largest bouquet of flowers I have ever seen outside of a hotel lobby. I have to step back to make room for the oversized arrangement between us. "Wow, thank you for taking them, Mrs. Ogden. I appreciate it."

"There's a card, but it's sealed." She watches Danny for a reaction out of the corner of her eye. She has to be wondering if this is my new boyfriend and if he sent the flowers. Admittedly, she's being a busybody, but we keep an eye out for each other in this building.

I take the vase but have to set it on the floor while I unlock my door.

"I can't thank you enough for accepting them for me. They must have taken up a ton of room in your place."

She shrugs. "They smelled nice."

Once Danny, myself, and my flowers are all crowded into my living room, I search for the mystery card. Not only is it sealed, but my name and address are typed on the front.

Danny is about to carry my suitcases into my bedroom and I wonder if it's his way of giving me a little unnecessary privacy. A Darlene-spy in his department tells me he isn't dating anyone; he doesn't have the same information about me. I want to reassure him, seriously doubting the flowers are from some secret admirer.

"I have nothing to hide from you."

He shrugs and carries my bags away anyway. When he returns, I'm sitting on the floor next to the vase, obviously confused.

"Who are they from?"

"Joel Rockhurst," I say.

"Joel Rockhurst? As in the CEO of JetStream, Joel Rockhurst?"

"Yeah." I nod, still studying the card. "And it's handwritten. I recognize his handwriting." I hold it up for Danny to see.

"What's it say?"

"'Bob told me why you left the conference early. I'm sorry for your loss. You and your father are an important part of the JetStream family.' It's signed by him for sure. I know his signature."

"I didn't realize Joel Rockhurst knew who your dad was. I've never seen him down on the maintenance floor."

"He didn't know who I was until recently. I got him an iced tea during the golf tournament." I study the gorgeous, fragrant flowers. "The man must really like iced tea."

I put the arrangement on my kitchen table, where it takes up so much room I'll have to move it to eat. I try moving it to the coffee table, but it blocks the TV screen. My already-tight living quarters just got that much more crowded.

Danny's cell phone rings. He answers but hardly says a word until he lets out a squeal, makes a fist and pumps it in the air. Nodding, he lets out a resounding "yes!" into the phone. "Of course I'll take the day off."

I shake my head at him. I have absolutely no idea who he's talking to. I mouth, "What, who is it?"

He proceeds to thank the caller profusely before he hangs up. Beaming, he looks at me. "Vivey, you'll never guess who's coming to town on Tuesday."

"Who?"

"Nick! And we're going to spend the day together. It would be fun if you joined us. What do ya say? Do you want to spend the day with Nick and me?" he asks enthusiastically. "Apparently my ex has an appointment in Savannah Tuesday and she offered to bring Nick to town."

"Ah, hmm, I'd love to, but I'll have to clear work?"

"Sure! It's going to be awesome. We should take him to the zoo. You know how much he loves animals."

"I do. I remember all the little animal figurines he had the last time he visited. His backpack was overflowing with them."

"Okay, so do what you can to clear your schedule. Vivey, it

would mean so much to me to have you there. I'd love for the two of you to get to know each other better."

"I'd like that too," I reply.

The three of us haven't spent much time together and knowing how much Nick means to Danny, I'm taking it as a positive sign for our relationship he wants me along.

"Great!"

It's Tuesday morning, zoo day with Danny and Nick. Turns out Bob had an out-of-town trip planned for today, so getting time off was easier than I expected. I'm free to enjoy some time with my favourite man and his son. Bob's only request was I check email at the end of the day and reply to anything urgent.

Hoping I look all right, I fiddle with the curls in my hair as I approach the gates. It's been a while since Nick's last visit and I want everything to go well today. I don't even remember the last time I came to the zoo. I didn't dress up too much, but I still wanted to look nice. I chose a simple, light green blouse, a pair of my favourite faded denim, cute black ankle boots, and an animal-print scarf to top off the look.

There is a large group of children in front, probably from a local daycare. I read online that there are special activity days for kids at the zoo and today happens to be Toddler Tuesday. As cute as they all are, I am looking for a different kid and a handsome man.

I look around, spotting Danny and Nick standing at the entrance, separated from the other groups, waiting for me to arrive. Danny flashes a smile at me as I approach. Nick stands right next to him, fidgeting with something in his hands. He appears to be zoo-ready, decked out in his favourite wolf hat and matching grey sneakers.

"*Excuse me*, you two handsome men over there! I'm looking

for a man and his son, but all I can find are you two *men*," I joke as I walk up to them. Danny, though normally stoic, cracks a small smirk while Nick giggles. I make a show of searching for someone else, spinning around in circles.

"Vivey!" Nick giggles, patting my legs, "it's me! Nick!"

Gasping, I squat down to his level. "Nick?! Nooo, you *can't* be Nick! I'm looking at a big boy in front of me!" I hear a small chuckle from Danny as he watches our exchange.

"I *am* a big boy," he claims, scoffing. A glowing smile still shows on his face. "I even picked out my own clothes today. See? I've got my alligator shirt on," he says, unzipping his hoodie.

Dramatically, I scan him up and down, picking up his hat and tousling his hair.

"And here I thought you stole clothes from your dad's closet." He laughs, looking back at his father to see if he agrees.

"Pretty sure those are my running shoes, young man." Danny winks at Nick as he extends a hand to help me up.

"Hey there," I say softly, cupping my hand around his.

"Hello," is all he says. Granted, he isn't much for public displays of affection. He interlocks his fingers with mine as Nick rushes over to hold Danny's other hand.

"Let's go!" Nick yells, tugging on us to move towards the entrance lines.

Getting through the entrance isn't so bad. The ticket salesperson is friendly and quickly has us on our way to security. I talk to Danny about my day as one of the guards searches my purse.

"Excuse me, ma'am," the security guard at the gate interrupts, holding up a bag from my purse with a few cookies inside. "You can't bring these in. I'm going to have to throw them away." I sigh but nod. It's been so long since I've been to the zoo, I forgot outside food isn't permitted.

"What was that?" Danny asks, mildly curious.

"Huh? Oh, I had made you guys a bunch of cookies as a surprise, but I forgot they don't allow outside food inside the zoo." I shrug it off, but Nick looks a little upset. "I left a lot of them at home. Maybe after we can stop by my apartment and grab you some." Seemingly satisfied, Nick looks at his dad again, eyes pleading.

"Sure, why not? We can do that," Danny confirms.

Sensing Nick is still a little bummed about the discarded cookies, Danny suggests we look at a map and decide where to go first. Nick searches for the wolf exhibit, spotting it like a hawk.

"You want to see the wolves?" Danny asks. I'm not surprised, considering wolves have been one of Nick's favourite animals for years now. Nick nods furiously.

"I wanna see if there's any babies! Like this one." He opens his hand to reveal a miniature wolf figurine. A child's infectious excitement never ceases to amaze me. Taking another look at the map, I notice the wolves are closer to the end of the trail.

"The wolves are here," I point out. "How about we walk the trail so we can see all the other animals along the way? Like the birds and alligators?"

His eyes light up at the idea of seeing alligators. Nick tugs Danny and me towards the mouth of the trail, where children clinging to ropes follow their teachers.

As we approach the alligator exhibit, Nick drops Danny's hand and rushes towards the glass barrier, pressing his face against it. He mimics the gaping jaws of a gator by snapping his fingers and thumb together.

Danny and I both let out a small chuckle. As we continue to walk along, Nick does the same with other animals. He growls at the cougars and sways from side to side with the monkeys. As we make our way to the birds-of-prey exhibit, Nick stretches his arms out wide and flaps them like wings.

"Hey, Dad, can you put me up on your shoulders? Please?" Nick asks.

Danny obliges, and from his new perch, Nick continues to flap his arms and squawk wildly.

"He's... the most energetic in his class," Danny comments, trying to keep Nick from falling by tightening his grip around the boy's legs. "Hold on, little buddy—don't be swaying those arms too crazy, now."

"Let's go, Dad!" Nick points to a sign with a picture of a wolf on it. "The arrow says that way."

I watch as Danny pulls Nick off his shoulders to hold him in his arms. He gives Nick a light peck on the forehead before putting him back on the ground. Nick runs ahead and Danny and I race to keep up.

"Daddy, look! Look at the wolves!" Nick's eyes widen, his little grey sneakers slap on the concrete as he half runs and half jumps the last few steps to the exhibit.

"Be careful!" I tell him as he nearly trips over a crack in the pavement.

"I am careful," he hollers back as he catches his balance, narrowly avoiding a face-plant onto the ground.

"You know, he likes you," Danny says, giving my hand a squeeze.

"Me? Oh, I don't know about that. He's such an open kid." I continue to watch as he howls at the wolves for their attention. A few of them look his way, but are unfazed.

"Not always." Danny looks at me. "He's shy around most adults, but with you, he seems at ease."

Nick is talking to another little boy who appears to be there with his class. The two of them laugh loudly, then howl together. The bright smile on his round little face is contagious. I smile, and so does his father.

Danny and I sit down on a bench a couple of feet from Nick

and Danny puts his arm around my shoulder, squeezing me close to him. "I'm glad you came with us today, Vivey."

"Me too, Danny, me too," I tell him, before standing up to join Nick in front of the enclosure. Sure, our relationship isn't perfect, but for now, I am happily enjoying this time with my loving boyfriend and his amazing son.

After we finish at the zoo, the three of us head back to my apartment so I can pack up the cookies I promised Danny and Nick. My heart melts a little when Nick gives me a big squeeze before he and Danny head out the door.

I guess it shouldn't surprise me Danny doesn't come back to spend the night. I suspect he's trying to milk every last second with his son before his ex picks Nick up.

What does surprise me is how little Danny and I speak over the next several days. I talk to him on the phone or we text, but only because I contact him about the storage garage we're renting together. It's almost as if our zoo day with Nick went a little too well and now he's putting a little distance between us. And it feels awful. He still hasn't given me a direct answer about moving in, so I'm going to take that as a yes and move ahead with the plan. I offer to meet him at his place the following Saturday so we can start packing. He reluctantly agrees.

When he opens the front door, I want to jump into his arms and take a week and a half's worth of sexual frustration out on him. He hugs me but stops there. The lack of kisses is unnerving, and I'm not sure how to react. I try to keep things upbeat and make myself useful.

I follow him around with my iPad as he points out the few things he's taking with him and what needs to go into storage. I make notes about the number of boxes we will need and sizes. I also start a separate section on repairs and sprucing up that will need to happen before his house goes on the market.

When we reach his bedroom, he stops the tour and finally

asks, "What are you working on there?" He glances at the screen.

"Just taking notes."

"Notes about what?"

"Packing, painting, stuff like that."

"Vivey, I got this. If you want to help a little, fine, but I know what I'm doing." I minimize my notes but don't delete them. "Okay, what do you want me to do?"

He looks around and it's clear he doesn't really have a plan. I bite my tongue and wait for his instruction.

"I guess start in the kitchen, pack stuff up in there."

"Okay, where are the boxes and packing supplies?"

"The boxes are in the garage, if that's what you mean by packing supplies."

The tension is building between us already, but the idea of just throwing breakables in a box is too ludicrous for me not to challenge.

"Do you have some bubble wrap or old newspaper I can use to protect stuff?"

He lets out a deep sigh as he puts hands on hips, a stance that says he is struggling to be patient. I'm not sure if it's with himself or me. I assume he doesn't have anything except boxes when he says, "Fine, start in the extra bedroom and I'll see about finding some newspapers."

I back out of the room to avoid pushing up against him since he's irritated. My eyes linger on his bed, the one I seriously doubt we will be using today if things keep going like this.

I make a ton of progress packing up Nick's room. It's functioning as a storage closet full of extra stuff rather than a well-used bedroom for Nick. As I sort through boxes of high school yearbooks and sports trophies, it hits me how little I really know about Danny's past and the things that matter to him. I've memorized every detail I've been able to observe since I've known him, but he's never really sat down and talked about his life to me. If I throw away this plaque he got for volunteer work in high school, would it matter to him? It's from Habitat for Humanity. I didn't realize he knew much about building a house.

From the other room, I hear Danny's phone ring.

"Hello?" he answers. His voice immediately softens. "Hey, little buddy. How are you?"

I know I shouldn't eavesdrop, but I can't help it. I move a little closer to the doorway. My suspicion that it's his son on the other end of the line is confirmed when I hear him ask, "Did the package I sent you arrive?"

Danny told me earlier he had shipped a care package out to Nick with some snacks, a pair of cool sunglasses he found, and a few comic books.

"I'm glad you liked the surprise. I wish I could be there to read them with you. You know how much I miss you, right?"

My heart breaks a little as I listen. I hear his voice crack as he talks to Nick. Whenever Danny shares things about his son with me, he's always very matter of fact. Maybe he's worried if he talks about Nick too much, he'll become emotional. Maybe he needs to be this tough "I've-got-it-all-together-guy" around me.

I envision the wall he's built. A wall too smooth to get a footing on and too tall to toss a rope over. Though lately, it would appear I've made a hole in it, or at the very least managed to shift a brick or two.

He switches into a proud-dad stance and I hear him compliment his son on a job well done.

"That's great! I wish I was there to see it. I knew you had it in you. I bet your teacher was proud of you. I'm so happy you called to share that with me. So, what's up for the rest of your weekend?"

There's a long pause. I imagine Nick is filling his dad in on whatever is going on at his end.

"I think about you all the time. I love you so much, Nick.

Don't ever forget that!" I can hear the sadness in Danny's voice and feel a little guilty about eavesdropping, but not guilty enough to stop. "You know I have to move away for a little bit and I won't be able to see you in person for a while, right?" He pauses, then continues. "I will write to you, and even though I'll be super busy, I want to plan for us to video chat at least once a week, okay?" He again pauses to listen. Finally, he adds, "I enjoyed our trip to the zoo too and yes, I promise the three of us will go again when I get back."

A few minutes later, I hear him end the call and I quietly walk towards his room. His back is to the door and he's leaning over his dresser with his head in his hands. I decide it's best to leave him to his thoughts, so I slink back to the other room before he turns and notices me.

Working in separate rooms is good for us. The tension dissipates and he seems grateful when I offer to go get more boxes and pick up some sub sandwiches for lunch. Of course, I also grab bubble wrap, shrink wrap, packing tape and labels from the store as well as sandwiches, chips, a six pack of his favorite beer and a bag of his favorite cookies. Before I check out, I toss a box of condoms in the cart too. I can never be too prepared.

I try to be subtle as I bring all the packing supplies into the house, and he doesn't mention them but glares to let me know I've gone overboard and they're unnecessary. I use our lunch time to ask him a little more about his past.

"I didn't know you could do carpentry."

He seems perplexed for a minute, then remembers the plaque. "Yeah, my family was big on doing charity work. Everybody had to do something. Building houses sounded easy to me."

This is the first time he's ever talked about his family to me. "You grew up in Florida, right?"

He nods as he takes a bite of his sandwich.

"Any brothers? Sisters?" I should already have this information, given how long I've known him, but it's never come up.

He drinks some beer before answering. "One brother."

"Is he still in Florida?"

Danny doesn't look at me; he concentrates on tearing open a bag of chips as he says, "No, he died. We were both in the military. He was stationed in Iraq. He didn't make it back."

My heart sinks and my throat is too tight for me to swallow another bite of food. "I'm sorry, Danny. That's horrible."

He shrugs without looking at me. "Comes with the job."

I don't know why he's being so cavalier—whether he never talks about it to anyone or is avoiding opening up specifically to me. The same sting of distance I've felt all week from him is there, between us. He's letting me into his life but only so far, only as much as he deems acceptable before he leaves.

I concentrate on my sandwich and wonder if maybe he's seeing this all more clearly than I am. And maybe he's right. Maybe we should just let New Orleans be a brief fling we had, and I should stop pushing him so hard.

But the doubts in my mind are quickly whisked away by the truth in my gut. We have a chance for something great here, even for a short time. I won't give up that easily. The reminder to seize the day is my soul's final gift from my dad, and I can't ignore it.

I change the subject. "Have you ever watched any shows about staging?"

"Like building sets for a play?" He shakes his head.

"No, staging is setting a house up to sell faster at the best price."

"Really? That's a thing?"

"Yeah, they have all these shows about what paint colors to choose and how to arrange the furniture and do things to make buyers see it as their home."

"Let me guess, you've watched them all." He's being coy, pretending not to know why I brought this up.

"I've watched a few. I mean, I've already got some great ideas we could do cheaply; a little paint, some flowering plants. I've seen them use spray paint to make old appliances look amazing."

And the patronizing glare is back...

"I'm just trying to help," I say.

But again, he pushes me away. "I know you are, but it's not necessary. You helping me pack some of this stuff up is enough."

He might be trying to tell me my help won't be needed after today, but I can play at the obtuse game too. I'm doing it for his good and mine, for what I know is right. I'm going to keep showing up and helping until he admits how much he needs me.

CHAPTER 12

I pack boxes all day on Saturday and when the sun sets, he offers to take me to dinner as a thank you. It's a sweet gesture and one I hope will lead to more romance, but I can feel it's also his way of evening out the score and letting me know he will do the rest himself.

Our conversation at dinner is neutral, Savannah news and weather, but I touch him a lot and he starts to loosen up. He holds my hand as we leave the restaurant, and as we're blasted by a chilly breeze, he puts his arm across my shoulders and pulls me close. There's a spark there, I can feel it; but unlike him, I can't turn it off.

Once we're parked in his driveway, he hesitates. We sit in silence and I feel like he's waiting for me to do something, except I don't know what. Is he waiting for me to announce that I'm going home? Because that's not happening. I can feel his reluctance; it only makes me want to work harder, to show him how great we could be together.

He finally opens his door and asks, "You coming in?" It's not exactly seduction, but I'll take it.

Things are no less strained inside. He seems lost amid the

sea of boxes. He doesn't offer, so I don't take off my jacket. Instead, I stand in the foyer, waiting for his next move.

He looks around, acknowledging all our hard work. "Thanks for your help today."

"Not a problem. I can help tomorrow too." As in, why don't I spend the night and we can get back to work tomorrow? I hope he gets the hint, because it's about as forward as I can get with him. Will I ever be able to completely relax when we're together?

"Vivey…" Taking my hand, he studies it as he rubs his thumb across my fingers. He uses a gentle tone for his brush-off. "I'm sorry. I shouldn't have let things get to this point."

I try to make things lighter. "What? Me helping you pack?"

He replies with his standard glare. "Us sleeping together. New Orleans was…" He struggles to find the words. I wait, not breathing, my throat closing around a lump of fear. "We were both hurting, needed each other, but…"

I can't let him do this. I won't let him finish dismissing me from his life. I grab on to a final thread. "Fine." My voice cracks with my lie. It's not fine, but I have to pretend it is if I want to stay in his life. "We can go back to being friends. Friends help each other move."

He looks up and shakes his head, possibly pleading for help from my dad to win this argument with me.

"That's just it. I don't want to just be friends. I feel great when I'm with you, but there is nowhere for this to go." When he looks at me, he sees the hope in my eyes. The only thing I heard was that he feels great when we are together. Anything after that, was lost to me. He holds me with his gaze. "I'm leaving. There's no way around it."

"So let's feel great together until you do."

I use his words against him but leave off until I figure out another plan. I lean into him, terrified that he will pull back. He doesn't, but it takes him a minute before he releases his resolve and his determination begins melting away. He kisses me as I peel off my jacket and toss it on the floor, and then reach for his.

I'm instantly flooded with a combination of joy and lust. I'm winning. And when he wraps his arms around me, he pulls me in close and I know I've got him just as much as he's got me. I gaze up and him. "Make me feel good. And please, please do not turn me down now because I couldn't take it."

My pleading is his undoing. He pulls me in tight, lifts me up and carries me toward the bedroom. *Yes! Oh, God yes!* The thrill of victory. I've seduced the man of my dreams.

"Hold on a sec," he says darting into the bathroom, me still in his arms. Opening the top drawer, he sees it's empty. Looking at me, he's waiting. He knows I can read his mind.

"I put them in your toiletry bag."

He pulls a string of three wrapped condoms from the bag.

I smile at him. "Three?" And I wiggle my eyebrows.

Danny tries but can't hold on to his power face, and he laughs. "If you're lucky."

I don't disagree because I can't. He's right. He pushes the hair off my neck and kisses me where he knows I love it. I dissolve into liquid.

"Relax. Can you do that for me?"

I nod my agreement and whisper, "You can feel free to nibble on my earlobes again." I let out a little laugh. "You know how I love that."

A puzzled look takes over his face. "Hmm, I'm pretty sure I've never nibbled on your earlobes before."

I tilt my head to the side as if I'm trying to recall a time. "Well, you have, in my fantasies," I tell him.

He smiles and shakes his head. "Seriously, Vivey, relax."

I'm seriously questioning my ability to do that. Relaxing is a foreign concept to me. Surrendering is the antithesis of my being.

We use two of the condoms that night and the third in the

morning. I definitely won't say the sex is dull, far from it. Like our relationship, it is intense. A night with Danny is exhilarating. There's lust and power struggles ending in blessed release, followed by regret (his), tears (mine) and finally, tenderness.

After a weekend of packing and pleasure, we are both ready to kick back and relax for a while. Danny orders us a pizza while I select a movie and grab a blanket off the bed. We snuggle up on the couch for the rest of the evening and simply enjoy being in others' company.

*

For the next few days, in my quiet hours alone in my apartment, my brain does what it always does: it organizes. I create a colour-coded, timeline/work chart. I painstakingly research how long it will take to perform each task to make his house more marketable, and then schedule them in the most efficient order and assign them. I print out two copies to take with me on Friday night when Danny's invited me to go over again.

I call Rach every morning on my ride into work so she can help me analyze everything going on between me and Danny.

"We're fighting about the paint again."

"Jeeeezus, not the paint again. Is he still mad you made him take the first color back?" Rach must have her own flow chart on her white board to keep track of all our issues.

"Probably. Last night, he took his bed apart and scraped the walls up as he carried it through the living room."

"Which is why you wanted to paint it last." Thank goodness I have Rach who understands the perfect logic of my plan.

"I know! I had to literally bite my lip and leave the room to keep from yelling 'I told you so.' But he knew. I didn't have to say it. Now I have to paint the same goddamned wall all over again. Third time!" These talks were supposed to calm me down, but I was getting all riled up again. Nothing grates on me more than gross inefficiency. "He fights me on everything. It's like he hates me now."

"He doesn't hate you. So you fight, then you get to make up. I'm sure much of it is the stress of him leaving soon."

I'm silent, but she's right. His leaving is the elephant in the room I can't control.

Her lack of further input on the subject tells me that even Rach is running out of answers.

I'm secretly thrilled when Danny dismantles his bedroom because it means he can stay at my place. I reason that maybe things will be better if we are away from the things we keep fighting about. But it turns out to be another grudging compromise. He comes home with me some nights but never brings a suitcase or even his toothbrush. And it doesn't improve our sex life much. I'm starting to feel like sex is now just another task on our colour-coded timeline.

One night, after a particularly vocal fight about how to arrange things in the storage unit, he lies in bed next to me but feels a million miles away. I want to apologize, yet I don't. I'm right, damn it. But I also want to try to grasp at his love, which I can feel him rapidly pull away from me.

"Arrange the locker any way you want," I say. It's not an apology but a concession.

He breathes a heavy sigh. "I don't care about the goddamn locker. And you're right anyway." The last sentence makes him sound completely defeated.

"Danny, I..." I start to explain my position again. He cuts me off.

"You're right, okay? I realize it, goddamnit. You're right about the paint and the furniture and the fact I need to take vitamins. You're right about the realtor and that I need to buy new work boots. You are right about everything."

"I just want to help you," I squeak out. I have a horrible tightness in my chest making it difficult for me to talk. I've been dying to hear those words, but not in this demoralized tone. I'm starting to realize that being right isn't everything.

He sinks back with a sigh. "I know you do, Vivey. I know." He stares at the ceiling, and I wait for the but-statement that will follow.

"What? Say it. Whatever it is."

"Don't wait for me."

I bite my lip and look down so he can't read my face. I'm caught. Now that it's clear he is leaving, I have been secretly planning our lives once he returns.

"I have a three-year contract. Do not wait for me." He stresses each word.

I don't answer because I won't agree to something I have no intention of doing.

He catches my lack of answer. "Fuck" slips out before he can stop it. He rubs his forehead as if I'm giving him a headache. "We never should have started this." He says it to the room, not me.

I can't face him now. I cry silently until I finally have to sniff. He looks over at me.

"Vivey." He brushes the tears away from one of my cheeks as I wipe them from the other. "I know you're not going to understand this, but I love you. I swear I do, but that's why I need you to agree not to wait for me."

"That makes no sense." I sniff again and try to curtail my crying. "You love me?" I grab on to that. "If you love me, we should be together."

"No." He reaches over and pulls me to him. "No, it doesn't mean we should be together. In our case, it means we should let go before we kill each other." He settles me against his chest. "Isn't it obvious I'm not the right guy for you? I don't want you wasting three years of your life not meeting the guy who *is* right for you."

"Is this because I'm pushy?" I don't know if he can read the terror in my voice, but I'm voicing my biggest fear: it's because of me, of who I am, we failed. "I'm literally pushing you away, aren't I?"

He breathes out and carefully chooses his words. "I have never met anyone who needs others less than you." He turns on the pillow to look at me. "I need to be needed, Vivey. I want to be needed. I want to be right sometimes."

I'm crying hard now. This really is the end of us, the end of my Danny dream, because we tried, and I failed. I have no counter arguments because for once, he's right. I curl up against him and let him hold me while I cry myself to sleep.

CHAPTER 13

*Y*ou know that sick feeling you get when you are still technically in a relationship but you know it's really already over? Danny and I are still a couple, but...

He goes to Charlotte to visit Nick for Christmas while I'm at Rach's trying not to spread my desolation all over her family gathering. I wish Danny and I could spend the holiday together, but I completely understand his desire to be with his son over Christmas.

Before he left, we exchanged Christmas gifts. I gave him a monogrammed duffle bag in brown leather, which he loved and used for his trip. I also wrapped up a couple of books I thought Nick would enjoy. Danny always talks about what an avid reader Nick is. Danny surprised me with a delicate silver locket embossed with flowers on the front. He said he purchased it in a quaint little antique shop he stumbled upon. It was dainty and beautiful and absolutely perfect! I love it. Truthfully, I didn't expect such a sentimental gift and my eyes filled with tears the moment I saw it. I'll never forget the way he softly brushed my hair to one side and kissed my neck as he put it on me. In that moment, it was as if all our problems melted away.

I'm still trying to wrap my head around the fact that this time next month, he'll be leaving for Saudi Arabia. Honestly, I don't even know exactly where that is, so I Google it. Apparently, it's 7,030 miles from here. Not exactly a weekend commute.

Rach's house is busy. Luis's family is here too, so there are now double the number of wedding-crazy, holiday-happy Puerto Ricans in the house. I hide out in Rach's room a lot, pretending to not obsessively check my phone for calls or texts from Danny.

I make an appearance at dinner, wishing it was socially appropriate to eat alone in the kitchen. I'm not sure if anyone else is buying my sham smile, but Rach isn't. She corners me in her bedroom and lures me out of my cone of sadness with her aunt's killer pie.

"I'm glad you're here."

"Seriously?" I smirk as I sit down on the bed. "I don't think I'm adding to the festivities."

Rach sits down beside me. "I would be worried sick about you if you hadn't come."

I lay my head on her shoulder and take another bite of pie. "Thank you, Rach. You don't need to worry about me, but thank you."

"I do worry about you because here's the thing: You think you're Wonder Woman, and you are probably the closest thing alive to her, but you're still human and you've had the shit kicked out of you these past few months. Even Wonder Woman gets to lean on her sidekick."

"She didn't have one."

"What? What about Steve Trevor?"

I laugh a little and shake my head at her ironic mistake. "Boyfriend and no, theirs was not a cry-on-my-shoulder kind of relationship." I soothe my raw emotions with another huge bite of pie. "I thought I wanted Danny, but I guess I only wanted the idea of Danny. He was right about one thing: We sucked as a couple." I say the words but know they lack sincerity.

Rach doesn't disagree.

"And I thought I wanted my dad to butt out of my life." I shake my head at the memory of all the times I told him to back off and pull in another shaky breath. "Now he has."

"You didn't make that happen. You're not that bloody powerful." She hugs me to her and rubs my back. "And I'm here for you. I'm not going anywhere."

"You're getting married, sweetie," I point out. "Luis will have you, and you'll have him." I lie back on the bed and set my empty plate on Rach's side table. I stare at the posters on the ceiling of her bedroom as I've done a thousand times before and contemplate my life. "My problem is I want a guy, but I don't."

"No, you want a man, but you don't *need* one. I always thought that was a good thing." Rach lies down next to me and grabs my hand. "And it is. You'll see, I promise. There will be someone, a smokin' hot male someone who can handle you, deal with how amazing you are. Someone who will appreciate you."

I lied. Deep down all I want, all I've ever wanted, is Danny. But I don't dare say that aloud. Instead, I say, "I'm glad you're so sure."

As the words leave my lips, I reach up and grab onto my locket, wishing it contained the magical power to fix everything. But I already know the only thing inside is a cheesy picture of Danny and I taken on my phone the night before he left for Charlotte.

"Are you going to his going-away party?"

I shrug. Maintenance is having a happy-hour get together at The Rail to send Danny off to the land of no liquor or unmarried women. Or maybe there are loads of unmarried women, they're just covered. It's Saudi after all.

"I'll probably stop by, but Bob's leaving for a major sales

presentation in Seoul the next day. I need to be at work early to make sure he has everything."

"I'll go with you if you want."

Apart from squeezing her hand, I don't reply. For once, I'm not making plans. My life feels too unstable and uncertain to plan… except for work. God bless my job.

⁂

My first day back to work after the holidays is finished and I am looking forward to getting home. Danny texted earlier to let me know he'd be getting back to town sometime today. As I approach my car, I see him standing next to it with a huge smile on his face. I'm usually out of the office before now, but I had some last-minute emails to send out that couldn't wait 'til morning. How long has Danny been out here, I wonder? His hands are suspiciously hidden behind his back.

"Hey, I wasn't expecting you to show up here. When did you get back?"

"Hi! Not that long ago. Just had time to swing by the apartment and drop off my stuff. I thought I'd surprise you," he says sliding a colourful bouquet of flowers out from behind him.

The flowers are wrapped in soft pink and lime green tissue paper and circled with a white satin ribbon. So pretty. "For me?"

"Yes, of course. Who else would they be for?"

"They're beautiful!" I touch the tip of my nose to the top of the velvety petals and inhale their sweet perfume. "They smell soooo good. Thank you." I lean up and give him a kiss.

"I missed you. I was hoping to spend some time with you tonight. My plan was for us to have dinner together, but on the way here, I got a call and I've picked up an extra shift at The Rail. So, I have to keep moving, but I'll see you back at your place later?"

"Absolutely. "

He kisses me one more time before hopping on his motorcycle. "Great, see you then."

We don't actually get to spend time together that night because I'm already asleep when Danny gets home. The next morning, I'm hoping we can have coffee together before I need to leave for work, but when the time arrives, he's sleeping so soundly I don't have the heart to wake him. I give him a kiss on the forehead and place a cup of coffee on the bedside table. I wrap a tea towel around the mug and set a saucer on top, hoping it will stay warm until he awakes.

For the next couple of weeks, the pattern repeats itself. He works long hours and tiptoes in well after I've gone to bed and I am up and out the door before he awakes. Our sex life has become non-existent, except for one early morning he woke up and joined me in the shower. But that felt more primal than sensual. Lately, it feels as if I could be standing butt naked waving my arms like a raving lunatic and the only attention I'd snare is that of a creepy drone seeking to capture America's funniest video from outside my bedroom window.

When the time comes, I do stop by Danny's going-away party, briefly and alone. Part of me wants to see everyone from maintenance, especially Darlene, and to be honest, part of me wants to see how Danny acts towards me around them.

If I need a final message that our relationship as a couple is officially winding down, I get it. He gives me a quick, friendly hug when I get there and moves on to make the rounds and talk to his friends. I don't think anyone else notices, but Darlene does. She comes over to me.

"Wanna talk?"

I shake my head.

She studies me for a moment. "You knew he was leaving, right?"

I nod.

"Hurts anyway?"

I nod again and she puts her arm around me, giving me a squeeze. "Call me anytime you need to talk, okay?"

I give her a weak, "Thanks" and stand next to her for what I hope is an appropriate amount of time before I beat it out of there. I wave to Darlene before I leave without looking back at Danny.

The next day, I have Bob packed up and in the air before noon. He's taking one of our newest, largest jets to demo for a Korean investor. As I watch him take off from runway nineteen, I glance across at the commercial terminal. Danny's there right now. I check the time on my phone. He's probably waiting to board his flight to New York where he'll connect with his flight to Riyadh.

I left him a note this morning, telling him goodbye and that I love him and probably still will when he comes back, whether he likes it or not. He still has half an hour until boarding. It would take me at least forty-five minutes to drive to the other side of the airport. Or… I could use the security clearance I keep for moving Bob's stuff around and take the direct route.

I commandeer one of the linemen from the JetStream ramp and ask him to give me a ride across. I have him drop me near Danny's gate. I've never abused my clearance before and can't believe I'm doing it now, but I submitted to everything short of an anal probe to get the security badge that I'm now flashing all over concourse C. I deserve to use it illicitly at least one time.

I spot Danny standing by the window, looking pensive. One of the stewardesses calls his flight over the PA system, warning passengers they will be boarding soon. He turns his gaze in my direction. Danny doesn't look overly surprised when he sees me approaching. He forces the weakest smile and nods.

"Of course you know how to get in here without a ticket," he says.

I flash my badge at him. "Of course."

I'm not exactly sure what I came to say, but I want us to part on a better note. We stand in uncomfortable silence for a few minutes and Danny leans back against the large concrete pillar behind him. He doesn't look at me, but finally speaks.

"You are amazing. You know that, right?"

I want to say, "But not amazing enough for you?" except that would keep us in the same place we have been for weeks now. So instead I say, "Thank you."

I touch his hand and he takes mine. "I know you don't see it, but you are still the most amazing man I have ever known."

He laughs. "Then you must not have known many men." He squeezes my hand. "I'm going to check up on you, you know, and I'll be home once a year." He looks out the window at the JetStream headquarters across the field. "I expect you'll be running the place by the time I'm back."

I chuckle. "I run Bob's life. That's enough for me."

"You say that, but…" Danny shakes his head. "No, you are going to go incredibly far Vivey; way too far for a grease-monkey like me."

I don't agree with him.

Other passengers have already begun to board, and when they call final boarding for his flight, my heart sinks in my chest. I want to grab hold of him so he can't go; instead, I stand in a daze. He bends to grab the handle of his carry-on and I let go of his hand. He leans in and gives me a quick kiss on the lips.

"I'll text once I'm settled. I will miss you, Vivey." That's the last thing he says to me before he turns and walks down the jet bridge towards the plane.

I call after him, "Love you."

I don't know if he heard me or not, but he doesn't turn around again. I want to stay and watch his plane take off, hang on to him until he's out of the same airspace as me, but my ride's waiting on the ramp.

I decide to take an afternoon off. Something I could do anytime Bob is out of town, but I never do. I'm in no mood for friendly office chatter today. I'm going to go home to sit on my perfect, oversized, tufted sofa and hug my pink chenille pillow. I'm going to have to face it alone sometime, feel the silence, move around without Danny in my way and miss him.

I'm sure much of the turbulence between Danny and me over the last couple of months was working through the idea our time was so limited. Facing the reality that as things were heating up between us, we'd soon be torn apart. Ten years of anticipation and now he's gone. I need time to grieve losing Danny and my dad.

I grab a ride back across the airport property to our offices where I stop by my desk to pick up a few things. An urgent email catches my eye.

It's from Carolyn Gauge, Joel Rockhurst's secretary. I open it.

Vivienne, I've set up a lunch meeting for you
and Mr. Rockhurst in his office Monday at
12:45. Please reply and confirm your
attendance.

What the hell? Lunch for me and Joel Rockhurst? This has to be a mistake. I call Carolyn. "This lunch meeting for Monday is for Bob, right? He's out of town, but he'll be back late next week. We can reschedule it."

"No. He specifically asked me to set up a lunch with you."

"Why?"

"Don't know, and he didn't offer a reason. You'll be here though?" She poses it as a question, but every one at JetStream knows that a request from Joel Rockhurst is really a command. No one tells him no.

"Uh, sure. I'll be there."

"Great. See you then."

I have no idea why he would want to have lunch with me, but I'm sure my brain will come up with a few million scenarios between now and 12:45 on Monday. My gut tells me this can't be good, but I'm not sure I can trust my gut right now. I still need to prepare to meet with the CEO. How do you prepare for the most random mystery meeting in the history of JetStream Aerospace?

I head home to my empty apartment. Walking through the door the realizations of the day hit me. I close the door behind me and press my back up against it. Then slowly slide down until my butt hits the floor. My shoulders drop as I let out a heavy sigh and without warning tears fall onto my cheeks. I want so desperately to believe this is all a dream. But it's clear by the way my heart aches that it isn't. I make no effort to wipe away my tears. Instead, I allow myself to feel, to grieve, and it hurts. It hurts deep in my bones. I reach up and touch my locket encircling it with my thumb, it feels like all I have left of him now. Danny's gone. He's really gone.

Fifteen or twenty minutes have now gone by, and my mind screams, "Pull it together, V." I lift my sorry ass off the floor as I give myself a few light taps on the cheek. It's my way of snapping out of self-pity. I know I'm stronger than this. Yep, I'm going to be okay. *Pity party over.* I wipe the tears from my face and stand. Flicking on the lights, I make my way over to the couch. With a firm hold on my pink chenille pillow, I take my phone and call Rach.

I share all about the mysterious meeting with Joel Rockhurst and how I can't stop thinking about Danny.

"It's so strange how things ended between Danny and me. So damn anticlimactic." The frustration in my voice is impossible to hide. "I can't help but think we should have had some stupendous goodbye, like the kind you see in the movies. Or, better still, when he saw me at his gate, he took me in his arms, swept me off my feet and told me he was staying. To hell with Saudi." I realize how cliché that sounds as the words leave my lips, but I don't care.

"I'm sorry, V." Rach tries to comfort me, but I keep talking.

"Now he's halfway around the world and I'm not sure what to do next. I waited for ten years to have my time with Danny—ten years. I know I need to move forward, Rach. I'm not sure I know how."

"You know what you need? A distraction. You should make a list." Rach knows me so well. "You should write out all the things you would want to have in your ideal man."

I think tall, dark, and handsome. Danny had those characteristics in spades. Rach continues as if she's reading my mind. "You need to forget about Danny and envision someone else now."

Rach is right. Plus writing out a list is never a bad idea.

I put her on speaker and place my phone down on the coffee table. "Hold on a second while I find a sheet of paper and something to write with." I grab a pad of lined paper and a pen from my desk drawer. Back on the couch, I write the title *My Ideal Man* across the top of the page. I insert a column of numbers from one to ten down the left side.

"Okay, I'm ready. Number one is easy: kind. My ideal man has to be kind. Actually, kind and polite." I go ahead and write kind and polite next to number one. "I know that's starting off with a twofer, but hell, it's my list.

"Number two, he's established. He owns his own house or condo apartment." I write that down and continue. "He doesn't need to be rich, but he should be financially stable. Being rich would be a bonus, but not a requirement."

"Okay, V, but this is supposed to be your ideal man, so it's all right to say he's rich. After all, it's just as easy to love a rich man as it is to love a poor one.

"True." I give a little laugh and scratch out *He's established* next to number two and replace it with *He's rich.*

"Number three is sexy," I tell Rach. "I have to want him. I know it sounds vain, but you said my ideal man. So, he's ripped —strong arms, six-pack abs, delicious lips, and great hair."

"So far, so good," says Rach. "Now, what's your number four?"

"Number four, he plays the guitar and he plays it well." Oh, how I love a guy who plays the guitar. I can't help but think what a natural Danny is. He's been playing since he was young and makes it look so effortless. I love listening to him play.

Rach adds, "He should also share your eclectic taste in music.

"True, good point."

"Number five, he owns a great car."

"Yes," says Rach. "Like a sexy Porsche, Lambo, or luxurious Jaguar."

"Exactly!" I respond.

"Number six…" I pause for a moment and announce, "Compassionate. I'd like the man I'm with to be compassionate. He should have a sincere heart for others. And that brings me to number seven: a sense of humour. I want to be with someone who makes me laugh, someone I can laugh with. Someone who puts a smile on my face.

"Sounds great so far, V, but I know what you're forgetting."

"What? What am I forgetting?"

"Your ideal guy better be organized. I can't imagine you living with a slob." Rach chuckles at her suggestion, which admittedly is quite accurate.

"Gosh, how right you are." And with that acknowledgment, I write the words *He should be organized* next to number eight.

"Only two more to go," I tell Rach.

"Number nine," I write, and simultaneously say aloud, "he has to want kids."

"Of course!" proclaims Rach. "You'll make a great mom one day."

"Number ten, last but not least, he should be romantic. The kind of man who will bring me flowers for no reason at all.

Someone who enjoys long walks on the beach. Eating out at the best restaurants. The type of man who will whisk me off on a mini-vacation I helped plan, of course."

"Without a doubt," says Rach.

I quickly add, "And, seeing as how we've already established this man is rich, none of that should be a problem. Oh, and if he's a little adventurous in the bedroom, that wouldn't hurt either. So, there it is. The top ten characteristics of my ideal man and then some." I let out a heavy sigh. "Now, all I have to do is find him."

"You will, V. I know you will."

CHAPTER 14

Saturday morning I wake up determined to keep myself busy. I'm up and out the door before ten. Running errands will help keep my mind off Danny and hopefully reduce the urge to check my phone every ten minutes. My first stop is the dry cleaners and then to the market to grab everything I'll need for the whirlwind of baking I have planned for tomorrow.

As soon as I pull into a parking space at the grocery store, my phone rings. It's Rach. "Hey, what are you up to today?"

"Just out running some errands. Why, what's up?"

"I read that the psychic fair is in town this weekend and I thought we could go check it out this afternoon. Might be fun. What do ya think?"

"You're only trying to keep me busy so I don't spend the day moping around thinking about Danny."

"Yeah, well, I don't know about that. I want to check it out. Will you come with me?"

"I thought you hated fortune tellers, considered them evil?" I ask.

"No, that's how my mom feels. I think you can't take them

too seriously. It's just for fun. So, what do you say? Will you come with me?"

"Yeah, sure, why not. Maybe someone can read my future and tell me what the heck Monday's meeting with Mr. Rockhurst is all about."

"Great! I'll text you the details. We can meet there? Say one o'clock?"

"Okay, sure. See you there."

I finish my errands and hurry back to my apartment to put all my groceries away before I head back out to meet Rach.

And as soon as I do, she wastes no time pushing me to a reading. "Check out the woman over there. She looks interesting. She's a psychic who uses tarot cards. You should have her read for you." Rach looks so invested, I can't say no.

As I sit across from the woman, I'm a little apprehensive but curious at the same time. What will she tell me? Can she *really* see my future? She hands me a deck of tarot cards and instructs me to shuffle them. I can't help noticing how long and slender her fingers are. Her manicured nails with deep red polish match the red flowers on her blouse perfectly. She appears to be about twice my age, and while she smiles and seems relaxed, there is an eerie seriousness about her. Perhaps it is the way she sits so straight in her chair or the sombre yet rhythmic way in which she speaks. After I shuffle the cards, she takes them from me and turns them over one at a time.

"Oh, I see a handsome man in your life, well dressed in a suit and tie. He appears to be in a position of authority. He's well-liked and very charming. Does this sound like someone you know?" she asks. I nod, tying the description to Joel Rockhurst.

"He will be instrumental in your career. You will learn a great deal from this man," she continues. "I also see he's connected to a man in your personal life; he approves of the man you will marry."

"What man? Is he going to introduce me to someone? Is that

what you're saying?" I'm a little surprised that Mr. Rockhurst is being positioned as my wingman, but hey, I'm not a psychic so I remain silent and allow her to continue.

"No, dear. I don't see him making an introduction, only approving of the choice you will make."

"That's interesting."

"I also see some sadness surrounding your immediate family; have you lost someone recently?"

"Yes."

"This person was very important to you. The Emperor card signifies the father or authority. A strong male energy, so I'm going to say your father or grandfather?"

"Yes."

"But the loss feels deeper. You've lost someone else too. Is this accurate?"

Damn, she's good! "Yes, someone I cared about deeply."

"I'm sorry. I can see in the cards the last few months have been difficult for you. I'm afraid I see more sadness on the horizon, but this time it will affect someone close to you. This person will need you to be there for them when this happens. They will lean on you quite a bit. But I sense you are strong and will shoulder much of their burden."

"I'm not sure I can take more difficult right now."

"You are strong, but even the strongest of us must take time for ourselves. You can't be all things to all people all of the time. Letting go doesn't come easy to you, but you need to learn to give up some of the control if you are to be successful in life. Take more time for yourself, find balance."

"Yes, okay. I understand."

"I'm not sure you do, but *you will*."

The emphasis she places on the last two words is eerie. I redirect. "What about the difficult time you mentioned? Whose burden will I be shouldering and when is this going to happen?"

"It will happen around the same time as your career change.

But don't worry, it's not all sadness. A few months from now, things will turn a corner for you in the romance department. Rather unexpectedly, I might add."

"Okay, but what events? What's going to happen? And to who?"

Gosh, she can't put that out there and not fill in the blanks, can she? Does a career change mean I'm going to lose my job? A knot forms in my stomach as I stare intently waiting for more information.

"Try not to worry. There are things in life we can't control, and this will be one of those things. I'm afraid our time is up for today. I have someone else waiting. But here's my card. Feel free to touch base again if you'd like another reading in the future.

I push my chair back and stand, looking around the room for Rach."Thank you," I say, handing her a twenty-dollar bill.

When I find Rach, she's looking over one of the vendors' tables. It's filled with books and crystals. "Hey, you ready to go?"

"Oh, yeah, sure. I was just killing time until you wrapped up. How was your reading?"

"Interesting. Apparently there's a career change on the horizon, and something unavoidable is going to happen, causing someone I care about to go through a difficult time."

"What kind of difficult time?"

"Not sure exactly, but she said I'm going to shoulder the burden for them. She was tight-lipped with the details. Oh yeah, and Mr. Rockhurst is going to approve of the man I will marry."

"What man?"

"I don't know. She made it sound like my love life won't be improving for a few months."

Rach nods but says nothing.

"So, how about your reading?" I ask her.

"It was more a past life thing than a future thing. Luis and I have lived multiple lives together. We are kindred spirits, always seeking out each other from one life to the next."

"Makes sense, you two have acted like you have known each other forever since the first time I saw you together."

"Yeah, what was funny, though, was the guy doing my reading kept going on about a lesson we needed to work through together, something we have yet to perfect. Guess we're stuck with each other until we figure out what the heck that's all about."

"What else did he tell you?"

"Honestly, nothing else makes a whole lot of sense. I kinda wish I did a future reading instead. I'm getting hungry. How about we get out of here and grab lunch somewhere?"

"Sure."

All day Sunday, I throw myself into baking for Rach's upcoming bridal shower. I crank out some high energy rock and roll on my Google speaker, a little louder than my neighbours likely appreciate, and set my worries aside. Getting down to business, I let chocolate brownies, red velvet cupcakes, and vanilla sugar cookies shaped into little brides' dresses occupy my mind and my hands. Well, that and a bottle of Chardonnay.

At one point, I catch myself belting out "Born to be Wild" by Steppenwolf, waving a tea towel around in the air and sliding my feet across the floor like a woman without a care in the world. Deep down, nothing is further from the truth but today is my escape from all that, a day I need to keep my sanity in check. So I sip, dance, and bake my heart out for the next several hours.

By the time the sun is setting, I have a refrigerator full of baked goods, an orderly kitchen, sparkling floor, and no doubt a little flour in my hair. Feeling rather accomplished, I remove my apron, pour the last bit of Chardonnay into my glass, let out a huge sigh and collapse onto the couch, completely oblivious to the fact I am not alone.

Whaaaat the hell was that! I instinctively jump up onto the couch. The iconic image of Tom Cruise doing the same on Oprah's couch flashes through my head. My eyes dart around the room, scanning the floor as quickly as I possibly can. I swear I saw something out of the corner of my eye, and it was no small thing. I think it was some sort of monster centipede. But where the hell is it now?

I'm completely vulnerable up here, and I'm barefoot! No way I'm getting down until I know what I'm dealing with. But I have to do something. I'm never going to be able to sleep tonight if I don't figure out what the heck that was and where the heck it went. And with the mysterious meeting happening tomorrow, I'm going to need sleep.

Taking another scan of the floor, I fix my eyes on the closet by the door where my tall black rain boots are. If I'm getting down from my perch on this couch in search of some dog-sized centipede, I'm going to need those boots.

I inhale so deeply my eyes suck back into my head. Counting down three, two, one, I bolt from the couch like a crazed lunatic and fling open the closet door, grab my boots and hop into them at lightning speed. I also grab the broom resting in the corner of the closet before swivelling around to scan the floor again. Reminding myself to breathe, I let out a huge exhilarating sigh as I say aloud, "I'm ready for you, you slithering, uninvited vermin."

Standing in the center of my apartment with a view down the hall to the bedroom, I see nothing. My blood races through my veins. Where the heck did it go?

I see it out of the corner of my eye again. I can't spin my head around quick enough. It moves so damn fast I can't make it out before it disappears under the linen-closet door. Okay, I got this. Sliding my boots across the floor as if I were skating on ice, one long stride after another, the broom outstretched in front of me with bristles pressed against the floor, I lean forward, grab the closet handle and swing the door open. "Aahhhhhh, good God, it's a mouse!"

It scurries out past my broom, making a sharp right in the opposite direction, heading straight into my bathroom and out of view again. Shit, that thing is fast! Arming myself with the broom across my body like a hockey player about to check someone into the boards, I move forward. I peer into the room; it's trying to hide in the corner behind the toilet, staring me down with its beady little eyes. My own eyes narrow as I stare back at it, my hands gripped so tight around the broom my knuckles turn bright red. Before I can contemplate my next move, the little bugger darts at me. Holy shit, it ran over the top of my foot—thank God for these boots! I spin around in time to watch it disappear under the couch.

Oh hell, no you don't. You aren't getting away from me. I race over, toss the broom down, grab hold of one end of the couch with both hands, and with brute force lift the end and drop it again. As expected, this gets the little bugger on the run again. He darts across the room and disappears under the buffet cabinet.

This could go on all night, I need to come up with a better plan. Clearly this mouse is powered by jet fuel. Outrunning him isn't going to work. I'm going to have to outsmart him.

Cookbooks! Of course.

I walk into the kitchen and grab a huge pile of hardcover cookbooks off the shelf. These will do the trick. I go back over to the buffet cabinet and press my cheek against the wall so I can peer behind to confirm he is in fact still there. And he is, huddled against the back wall. Wait, what? That was weird, did I just gender a mouse? I give my head a shake, take the books one at a time, and form a border all around the cabinet. Now there is no space under the cabinet to which the mouse can escape—it's trapped. The rush of my victory is swiftly extinguished when I realize I now have to get him out of there and out of my apartment.

I collapse back onto a side chair as I endeavour to come up with a clever plan. Before I can, there's a knock at my door. My neighbour from downstairs stands with a concerned look on her face.

"Is everything okay, dear?" she asks.

"Oh yes, Mrs. Kelley. Everything is fine. Why do you ask?"

"I was watching TV and I heard a huge bang overhead. It sounded like something came crashing down."

"Of course, the couch. I'm sorry about that. I wasn't thinking. I was chasing a mouse and it ran under my couch. I tried to scare it out by lifting and dropping the end. It worked, but I wasn't thinking about the noise I was creating."

"A mouse? Oh my. I've never had them in the apartment. We do get them in our storage unit in the basement occasionally. We always have traps down there and Mr. Kelley checks them from time to time. Where is this mouse now?"

"I've trapped it under my buffet cabinet. I was trying to think of how I'm going to get it out from there when you knocked on my door."

"I think I still have some traps left. Let me go downstairs and get you one. They're the sticky ones. If you can get it onto the sticky pad, I can have Mr. Kelley come up when he gets home and remove it for you."

"Okay, but I hate to kill it."

"No, dear, we won't have to kill it. That's what the sticky traps are for. The mouse will get his feet stuck to the trap and won't be able to move. Mr. Kelley can remove the mouse from the pad and set it free."

"Oh, that's perfect. Thank you so much, Mrs. Kelley." I notice she's staring at my boots.

"Are those your mouse-hunting boots?" she asks.

"Yeah, I guess so." I shrug. "There was no way I was chasing that thing around my apartment barefoot."

Mrs. Kelley smiles as she turns towards the stairwell. A few minutes later she returns with the trap. "Here you go, dear. Just place a dab of peanut butter or cheese in the center of the pad and place it where the mouse is hiding. Then check back and call me when he's stuck. I'll get Mr. Kelley up here to retrieve it for you."

"Wonderful, thank you so much. I really appreciate it."

"You're welcome, dear."

Alone again, me and the mouse. I remove the trap from the plastic wrap and place it on the kitchen counter. Grabbing a spoon and some peanut butter, I place a tiny amount in the center of the tray as Mrs. Kelley instructed. I know I will need to be quick when I place this. I kneel down in front of the cabinet, and in one smooth and rapid movement, I slide one of the cookbooks to the side, insert the trap behind it, and slide the book back again. There, it's done.

Feeling confident, I remove my boots and put them back in the closet with the broom. I make myself a cup of tea because the only thing left for me to do now is to wait. As I'm stirring my tea, it dawns on me that earlier the apartment was getting so warm from the oven I'd opened the balcony door a crack to cool it down a bit. That must be how the little bugger got in. I'm sure I read somewhere mice can climb walls or maybe the trees out back provided the little bugger access. Guess I'll never know for sure, and it doesn't matter how he got in as long as I can get him out.

About thirty minutes have gone by. My tea is finished and I decide it's time I check the trap. Getting my cell phone and turning on the flashlight app, I kneel in front of the cabinet, ready to peer underneath the moment I slide one of the cookbooks away. Somewhat terrified the mouse has not been trapped and is waiting to pounce at my face, I hesitate. Three, two, one...

I push one of the cookbooks aside, leaving about an inch of space to peek in. The flashlight works, illuminating the entire space under the hutch—and there, in the middle, is my nemesis immobilized on the pad.

CHAPTER 15

My alarm goes off at five-thirty a.m. on Monday, about one hour earlier than usual, giving me some extra time to get ready. One would think that after my baking marathon and mouse fiasco last night, I would have slept like a baby. But, how could I? I tossed and turned most of the night, preoccupied with the fact that today is the day of my mysterious meeting.

After my shower, with my towel still wrapped around me, I stand in my closet looking over my entire wardrobe, agonizing over what to wear. How do I decide what to wear when I have no idea what I'm dressing for? Should I wear a dress, a tailored suit, a skirt and blouse? Should I wear my hair up or down? I frantically pull one option after another from the closet. Why the heck does Joel Rockhurst want a meeting with me anyway?

I try on several outfits and a pile of rejects fills my bed before I decide to keep it simple and go with black dress pants and a black-and-white polka-dot blouse. Then I neatly return all the clothes I chose not to wear to my closet. I do my makeup and hair, deciding up is best, and whip up a protein shake for breakfast. I can't imagine trying to stomach anything else this morning. I down my shake and check my phone for the third time this morning. But there is no word from Danny. Not even a quick text to say he's arrived safe. As badly as I want to text him, I don't. Instead, I remind myself to stay focused.

Grabbing my purse and keys, I head out the door. I stop into I-Sales to get the Monday morning report done for the sales meeting at ten and check and answer important emails that came in for Bob over the weekend.

About ten to ten, Ted pops by my desk as he usually does Monday mornings to grab the sales report before heading into the meeting. "Morning, Vivienne. Got the report ready for me?"

"Yes, it's all ready for you. Oh, and Bob asked me to remind you to make sure you email him the minutes from the meeting today."

"Yeah, yeah," says Ted. "Bob worries too much. He already reminded me twice before he left. He always gets a little antsy as we get closer to the end of the month. Thanks again for this," he says, holding up the report as he walks away.

I get back to answering emails and following a few other odds and ends, and before I know it, it's time to go. I log off my computer and return everything to its proper place. I stand and look down at the small picture of my dad and me sitting on the corner of my desk. I grab the picture and toss it in my purse. Maybe Dad will bring me luck.

I give myself plenty of time to get to the JetStream executive offices so as not to be late for my mysterious 12:45 lunch meeting. And I'm not. I arrive ten minutes early, which gives me plenty of time to visit the ladies' room and touch up my lipstick before taking a seat in the reception area. Carolyn Gauge, Mr. Rockhurst's secretary, greets me with a big smile. "Thanks for coming in, Vivienne. Mr. Rockhurst is looking forward to meeting with you. Please go ahead and grab a seat. I'm sure he won't be too long."

"Great, thank you."

I sit, crossing my legs one way and then the other as I shift the purse from my lap to the seat beside me and back to my lap again. I pick up the closest magazine and pretend I'm interested in what it says. Meanwhile, all I can think of is why the heck I'm here in the first place.

Joel Rockhurst is the youngest CEO JetStream Aerospace has ever had. When he was appointed to the position a little over a year ago, someone said he was thirty-three. So that would make him nine years my senior. Not that I'm counting or anything. Besides being the youngest CEO JetStream has ever had, he's without question the hottest. In fact, as rumour has it, his nickname is Mr. Hotness. It's a name I've heard floating around on more than one occasion. Apparently, "Mr. Hotness" was bestowed on him by some of the ladies in the accounting department soon after he took over as CEO and it stuck. Never used in his presence, of course.

The phone on Carolyn's desk rings and she is engrossed in conversation when Mr. Rockhurst steps out from his office. "Vivienne, I'm so glad you could stop by. Carolyn, please hold my calls. Vivienne and I have a lot to discuss." Carolyn nods and he motions for me to lead the way into his office.

"Hello, Mr. Rockhurst. It's nice to see you again," I say as I stand and walk towards him.

"Please come in and take a seat. I'm sure you're curious as to why I've asked to see you today?"

"Yes, I am curious. But before I forget, I want to thank you for the lovely flowers and thoughtful note you sent to my apartment after my father passed away. That was very kind of you."

"It was my pleasure. I meant what I said. Your dad was an important part of the JetStream family. He will always be remembered for the valuable contributions he made to this company. Although I never had the pleasure of working with him personally, few have the stellar reputation Mike Ramsey has around here."

"Thank you for saying that. I know it wasn't an easy decision for him to leave, he enjoyed his time here. Now Mr. Rockhurst, please tell me how I can help you?"

"Well, after meeting you at the company golf tournament, I asked around about you. It seems you're very respected around the I-Sales offices and your boss, Bob Brockhaus, has nothing but praise for the job you do over there. He says you are always one step ahead of him."

"That's nice to hear."

"I was wondering, Vivienne, where do you see yourself five years from now? Do you have any aspirations for your future with JetStream?"

"Honestly, I'd welcome the chance to challenge myself more should the opportunity arise." Does this mean I'm not getting axed?

"Well, what if I told you there may be an opportunity for you in the very near future? Carolyn has told me she'd like to spend more time with her family, and that means stepping down from her position as my executive assistant. While this is not a formal interview, I wanted to reach out in case you might be at all interested in stepping into the role?

"Seriously?!" That sounded way more surprised and squeaky than I intended. But Carolyn never said anything to me.

He chuckles. "Yes, seriously."

"Yes! I mean, absolutely. I would definitely be interested."

"Well, why don't we go out and grab some lunch? It will give us a chance to get to know each other and discuss the position."

Damn, he's charming. My cheeks flush. "Sounds great" is what I say, but HOLY CRAP is what I'm really thinking. Executive assistant to the CEO is definitely a step up from my current position, and I'm sure it comes with a nice raise too. Granted, it's sure to involve longer hours and more responsibility, but I'm up for the challenge. And with Danny away in Saudi Arabia, extra time won't be a problem. In fact, the less time I have to sit around my apartment missing him, the better.

"How does Zunzi's sound?" he asks. Zunzi's is a popular lunch spot in Savannah. The food is amazing and I've often called them to cater interdepartmental meetings and events.

"Sure." I stand and wait for him to come out from behind his desk.

"After you," he says, again motioning with his hand for me to take the lead. "I'll drive."

As we exit his office, he asks Carolyn to call Zunzi's and have them reserve us a table.

"Sure, Mr. Rockhurst, I'll do that right away. Enjoy your lunch," she says.

We make small talk as we head towards the elevator and out to the parking garage. I expected it to be a bit awkward and instead find he's rather easy to talk to. He is a true gentleman, opening doors for me as we work our way through the halls and out of the basement to the garage area. As we reach his parking spot, I see his sleek, jet-black Porsche 911, so clean you can see your reflection in the paint. He opens the passenger door for me before walking around the front of the car and getting into the driver's seat.

"Great car, how long have you had it?" I'm thinking it can't be long; to say this car is spotless is an understatement. And it still has that new-car smell.

"About a year now. She's real fun to drive."

I smile as I reach for my seat belt and buckle myself in. I've never been in a Porsche before and I try to act casual and not let on how in awe I am. The black leather seats curve in at the sides, caressing and enveloping me in comfort. Everything about the interior is luxurious and rich, right down to the glossy mahogany-wood accents. I resist the urge to reach out and slide my fingers across the dash. The roar of the engine only serves to intensify the experience as we peel out of the garage and onto the street.

Once we arrive at the restaurant, the hostess recognizes him. "Hello, Mr. Rockhurst. Welcome. Carolyn called and told us to expect you and Miss Ramsey. Your table is ready, please follow me."

She walks us over to a table near the window and asks Mr. Rockhurst if it's suitable; he smiles and assures her it is. He pulls out my chair for me before taking his own seat across the table. There is always a wait at Zunzi's. At least that's been my experience, but not today. He seems to have clout here. A few of the staff members have already made a point to say hello and others have acknowledged him with a quick wave from across the room.

He wastes no time looking over the menu. "Think I'll have the Godfather, it's a great sandwich. I've had it before and it comes with their signature Shit Yeah Sauce, which is to die for."

My mouth waters as I read the menu, but I think I'll keep it simple; no fancy sauces that could accidentally find their way onto my blouse. I decide on a whole-wheat wrap with chicken and veggies as the waitress returns to take our order. Mr. Rockhurst also asks her to bring us a bottle of white wine.

As soon as the wine arrives at the table, he asks, "May I pour you a glass?"

"I don't usually drink during the workday, but I guess seeing as how you're the CEO..."

"And you wouldn't want to turn me down, right?" He raises and lowers his eyebrows in a playful fashion as he fills my glass.

"No, I guess not." I laugh. "Thank you."

After pouring himself a glass, he tells me all about how much he enjoys working with Carolyn, and what a wonderful job she does managing his day-to-day schedule and correspondence. The way he talks about her makes me realize I have some big shoes to fill if I am to replace her.

I share a little of my background with the company and the pertinent information about my current responsibilities and skills—hoping he will conclude I'm a worthy candidate for the position.

We also talk about hobbies. He expresses his love for fine art and how he enjoys visiting galleries when he's travelling. I, of course, make sure to mention how much I love to cook.

"Maybe I'll have a chance to sample some of your cooking one day."

"Maybe. I've been known to bring a dish or two to the office from time to time."

"Your boyfriend must appreciate you being such a good cook."

I haven't said I have a boyfriend—he's fishing, right? Oh my God, is he wondering whether or not I'm single?

"Ah, well, that's kinda complicated. I'm not sure I have a boyfriend at the moment." Desperately wanting to move off this topic, I ask, "So, did you grow up here in Savannah?"

"No, I actually grew up in California. My folks still live out there."

He goes on to tell me a bit more about his background and the more he talks, the more intrigued I become. His clean shaven face reveals his flawless complexion and his intense green eyes seem to possess some magical gravitational pull that's drawing me in physically. I can feel my body leaning towards him. And did I mention he looks killer in a suit? I can picture him on the cover of *GQ* as one of Savannah's hottest married men. I manage to break my gaze for a moment to look down at his left hand for the telltale sign he's unavailable, but there's no ring. What? Wait. No. How did I miss that? Did he and his wife, the former Miss Georgia break up? Does this mean he's single?

He's still talking, but I don't think I've registered a word he's said for the last two or three minutes. Realizing I've been daydreaming, I jolt myself back to the present moment, straighten my posture, and ask, "What is it you value most in an executive assistant?" praying he didn't notice my trip to Lala Land.

He doesn't miss a beat and answers, "Loyalty. Carolyn is loyal to me, always has been, and that makes my life so much easier. I don't need to worry about whether or not she has my best interests at heart, I know she does." He continues, "Dedication is a close second. If my assistant is dedicated, things rarely fall through the cracks—and that's critically important at this level."

"Well, working with Bob, I mean Mr. Brockhaus, has certainly provided me with the opportunity to hone those skills." Seriously though, some days it's as if I'm Bob's third arm.

Before we know it, two hours have passed. The waitress asks, "Will there be anything else for either of you today?"

He looks at me and I shake my head before he says, "No, thank you, just the check please."

As he's paying, he looks me in the eyes and says, "I've enjoyed our lunch today, Vivienne. It's been wonderful getting to know you."

Seriously? Mr. Hotness, the pleasure has been all mine. "I enjoyed it too. And thank you for lunch, it was delicious."

"It was, wasn't it? The food here never disappoints. Once I get back to the office, I'm going to tell Carolyn to email you the outline for her position and a link to an online application you can fill out."

"Great, I'll watch for it. Do you know when Carolyn is going to step down or when you might be looking to fill her position?"

"She told me she'd like to leave in a few weeks. I'm hoping to conduct formal interviews this coming week so she will have time to help train her replacement before she goes."

As we leave the table, he puts his hand on my lower back to

guide me towards the door and I picture Danny and the way he would sometimes do the same. God, how I miss him.

On the way back to the office, Mr. Rockhurst shares a few more details about what he expects from his executive assistant and does a good job of selling me the position. Not wanting to get my hopes up, I ask, "How many people do you expect to interview?"

"I have asked Carolyn to post the position in our company's newsletter which goes out later this week and also notify the head-hunting agency we work with. I expect there will be a few applicants from outside, but I'd like to hire internally if the right person is interested." He smiles but keeps his eyes on the road.

"Well, you have piqued my interest and I look forward to receiving Carolyn's email. Perhaps it would be a good idea for me to suggest she and I meet sometime this week. I'd love to get her perspective on the job."

"I think that's a wonderful idea. Why don't you discuss it with her when we get back to the office?"

"I will," I reply as he pulls back into the parking garage.

Mr. Rockhurst demonstrates again how gentlemanly he is as he once again opens my car door and stretches his arm, motioning for me to take the lead back to the office. Add rich, smart, kind, and considerate to his list of qualities. It's no wonder Mr. Hotness is taken. Or is he? As soon as I get back to my desk, I'm going to have to check in with Darlene. If anyone knows the scoop, she will.

Back in the office, Mr. Rockhurst thanks me again for meeting with him and leaves me to chat with Carolyn as he heads to his office, closing the door behind him.

After the chat, I swing back by I-Sales and pull the picture of Dad and me from my purse, returning it to its rightful spot on my desk. It may have brought me luck afterall.

I give Darlene a call.

"Listen, Darlene, I was wondering if you knew the scoop on

Mr. Hotness. I mean, Mr. Rockhurst's marital status? I knew he was married, but today he wasn't wearing a wedding band."

"Oh, you noticed that, did you?" She laughs into the phone. "And where were you that you happened to notice that?"

"He asked me to lunch. Apparently, Carolyn is quitting and he's looking to replace her. He said he'd been asking around and thought I might be interested in applying for the position."

"Wow, what a terrific opportunity for you. I hope you told him you were interested."

"Yes, of course—now back to my original question. Do you know if he's still married?"

"Well, I did hear she left. A couple of months back. Something about her missing California and him not being home enough."

"Interesting. Okay, thanks, Darlene."

"Be careful with that one, Vivienne, he's a real charmer."

For a brief moment, I'm reminded of the list Rach and I made: *My Ideal Man.* I can't help but think about how Rockhurst is fulfilling that list. But there's my rule about not dating guys I work with. And even if that wasn't a rule, there is one glaring shortfall when it comes to Joel Rockhurst. He's *not* Danny.

After I hang up, I check my email and there, as promised, is the link to the job posting.

CHAPTER 16

The last few days have flown by and today was my formal interview for Mr. Rockhurst's executive assistant position, which I'm confident I nailed. In fact, I feel so good about it that I decided to make myself a gourmet dinner of tangy honey-glazed chicken thighs with roasted peppers and zucchini to celebrate. Grabbing my oven mitts, I pull the chicken and vegetables from the oven; they look flavorful. The sweet and savoury aroma fills my apartment and I'm about to take my first delicious bite when Rach calls.

"Hey."

"Hi. Guess what?"

"What?" I ask

"Luis and I put a deposit down on our wedding venue this morning."

"Really? That's great."

"It is, but there's still a lot to do, and I'm sure the next few months will fly by."

"I hope I find a man before then. How many eligible bachelors are on the invite list? Luis got any sexy single cousins I don't know about?"

Rach laughs. "Not any I'm aware of but, I'll keep a lookout."

"Sounds good."

"By the way, Viv, I'm looking forward to this Saturday."

"Yeah, me too. Almost everyone I invited has said they're coming, except for Bonnie. It's her aunt's fiftieth birthday bash that night. She said she'd much rather be at your bridal shower, but her mother would never forgive her if she blew off her aunt's party. Her mom's been planning it forever."

"That's okay. There'll be plenty of us gals there to party it up. I know you keep saying you have everything under control but are you sure I can't come over early and help you get set up?"

"Nope. It's your shower, no way I'm having you lift a finger. Just be here at twelve-thirty, ready to party."

Rach laughs. "Okay, I can handle that. If you change your mind, I've got nothing else going on earlier in the day and am happy to help out. It's not like it's a surprise or anything."

"I know that. But, as your maid of honour, it's kinda my job to throw you a kickass shower. So, leave everything to me."

"You're the best. I gotta run, Luis is walking in the door. Chat later?"

"Sure. Tell Luis I said hi and remind him my place is off-limits to him Saturday afternoon."

Normally, I would have jumped in and told her about how well my interview with Joel Rockhurst went, but my dinner is cooling off and it looks heavenly. I will update her later. The chicken doesn't disappoint; it's salty and sweet with a hint of ginger. Soooo good.

Before I can finish eating, my phone lights up and I almost fall out of my chair. It's a text from Danny! I'm in such a rush to see what it says, I accidentally tip over my water glass, which spills over the side of the table onto my lap. I grab my napkin to slow down the rest of the water and snatch up my phone.

Hi, Viv. How r u?

Really, that's all he has to say? No *"sorry I haven't been in touch?"* He could have been dead for all I know. I take a deep breath and text back.

Good. You?

I'm not about to give him the satisfaction of knowing how desperately I've wanted to hear from him.

*Good. It's been busy, lots of work, long hrs.
I've thought about you often and I've wanted
to reach out, but I wanted to give you space.*

Space 4 what?

To move on.

Oh.

And so, have you?

*Have I what Danny? Moved on? Are you
asking if I'm seeing someone?*

*I guess I am. Though I'm not sure I'm ready
for the answer.*

*Well I'm not. I've been busy too. Things at
work, planning Rach's shower etc.*

I miss you Viv, a lot.

It's exactly what I want to hear, but I don't know how to respond. So I don't. I put the phone down and grab some paper towels and start mopping up the water. My phone lights up again, and again. What do I say to him? I sit staring at my phone for what seems like forever, although it's only been a couple of minutes.

I pick up my phone and read his texts.

Are u still there?
Viv?
Please respond.

I write:

I'm here. I miss you too Danny, I don't
understand why you couldn't have texted me
sooner. It would have been nice to know you
arrived safely. You could have at least
reached out to let me know that. It's been
weeks without a single word.

The message pings back:

I know, I'm sorry. Leaving you was hard.
Harder than I expected. I think about you
every day. Things have been a bit crazy here
and we have to pick up and move camp. I
don't know if I'll have service where we are
going, and I wanted to get a message to you
in case I don't have the opportunity again for
a while.

Moving camp? Why?

There's been a lot of violence in the area and
the company I'm working with wants to move

us before there is any more escalation.

That doesn't sound good.

*I'm sure it will be fine. Moving us is a
precaution. I have to go now. They are getting
ready to roll out. I just needed you to know I
haven't forgotten about you.*

Please be safe, Danny.

Yep.

*I'm glad you texted me. I miss you. Please
don't go so long before I hear from you again.*

I'll try. Viv—I love you.

And that is the last text I receive. I want to say I love you back, but my fingers freeze.

As I sit here looking at the sopping wet paper towels and what remains of my dinner, now cold and unappealing, I'm unsure of what to think. Maybe Danny only reached out because the situation in Saudi is tenuous? Is that what is driving his emotions? Has he really thought about me every day? I want to believe he meant what he said, but if he has thought about me every day, if he does love me, why would he have waited so long to reach out?

I clean up the kitchen and get ready for bed. Thoughts of Danny and me swirl around in my head. And I crave him all over again. Stretching out on my bed, I close my eyes. Within minutes, I drift off to the only place I want to be, in his arms.

His lips are warm and sweet and his breath intoxicating as he circles my mouth with his. My head sways back and forth. I close my eyes and caress his head with my hands as if doing so will somehow ensure he won't pull away. Everything else around us fades, it's only us. I slide my fingers through his hair; my God, he has exquisite hair. He moans in approval as I tug and twist his locks between my fingertips.

Gently biting down on my bottom lip, he holds it between his teeth, but only for a moment before he slowly releases, teasing me. He pulls me closer to him; our bodies melt together as his strong hands gently glide over my shoulders and down my back. His kisses move to my neck, his teeth tugging on my earlobe as he blows into my ear. He unzips my dress with one hand while clutching my thigh with the other. This is so unlike me, letting him take the lead like this, but I'm thoroughly enjoying every second of it. My whole body is tingling.

Noooooo, the noise of my alarm jolts me back to reality. Damn it! I check the time: six-thirty a.m. How is it that a dream that felt like a few minutes took the whole damn night? I grab my phone off the nightstand. I need to confirm those messages with Danny last night were real and not an earlier part of my dream. There they are: *I'll try. Viv—I love you.*

His words sink in, and just like that, I'm pulled back into his vortex and my head is spinning. I'd been doing so well putting him out of my mind lately, trying to move on. Could it be I've underestimated the power he still has over me?

✳

It's the night before Rach's bridal shower and I'm up late icing the little sugar cookies I made for tomorrow. I've already cut up all the veggies for the vegetable platter, made the salads, the tiny sandwiches and pulled together a four-layer nacho dip Rach loves and some spinach dip for the pumpernickel loaves I made earlier today. Most of the apartment is already decorated; all I need to do in the morning is make the punch. Feeling rather satisfied with all I've managed to accomplish, I turn out the lights and head to bed.

By noon the next day my apartment is buzzing with conversation and laughter as Rach's family and friends await her arrival. Twelve-thirty comes and goes, and there is no sign of Rach.

About ten minutes later, her mom, Lucca, asks, "What time did you tell Rachel to be here?"

"Twelve-thirty. She must be running a little late," I respond.

"You'd think she'd be on time for her own party," Lucca says.

It's after one o'clock and I suggest a game of bra pong to occupy ourselves until Rach arrives. But honestly, I'm worried so I slip into my bedroom and call her. My call goes straight to voicemail. She must be driving—that's good, I tell myself, she'll be here any minute. I return to the living room and occupy myself by setting out a few more snacks and topping up the punch bowl with ice.

Two o'clock passes and the chatter has cooled. Everyone is wondering where the guest of honour is. A couple of people are texting on their cell phones, trying to reach her. Her mom's face is expressionless as she looks around the room and goes to stand by the window. I pick up my phone and try to reach Rach, again. This time I don't hide in my room. Voicemail. This is so unlike her.

Then her aunt Maria says. "I've got her."

I turn off the music and we wait in silence for her aunt to update us. Maria's eyes are wide and she's shaking her head from side to side. She sits down on the couch with her cell phone glued to her ear and says, "Okay, I'll tell them. Yes, I understand—No one would expect you to—Yes, yes, okay—No, don't worry about that now. I love you." She puts the phone down and looks at all our faces staring at her.

"Well!" says Lucca. "Where is she?"

Maria proceeds to tell us all that Luis had been in a terrible car accident and Rach received the call as she was leaving to come here. "She was frantic and she's sorry she didn't think to call you, Vivienne. She wanted to get to the hospital to be with Luis. They have taken him into surgery and she's staying put until he comes out. I told her that none of us would expect her to be anywhere else right now and she shouldn't worry about that." She takes a breath, puts her phone in her purse, and stands. "Lucca, come on. I'll drive you to the hospital."

"Yes, you go. Rach will want you there. I'll put a few things away and head over too," I tell her mom.

"I'm going too," says one of her cousins. Followed by, "Me too" from someone else. Before I know it, about a dozen people are grabbing their things and running out the door. A couple of Rach's friends from work stay back and help me put the food away before they too grab their things and head out. I'm relieved that no one has lingered since I want to get over to the hospital myself and be there for Rach.

As soon as I walk through the emergency room doors, I see them—but not before I hear them. Rach's family doesn't have volume control; it's either loud or louder. They are all talking over one another, trying to figure out what is going on and whether or not Luis is out of surgery. Of course, the hospital staff isn't willing to give out any information, as none of them are family to Luis. One nurse calmly tries to explain how everyone needs to go out of the emergency room and back in through the main hospital doors.

I walk up to the courter, smile, and nod at her. "Thank you," I say, and wave my hand towards the door. "Come on, we've gotta go find Rach. She'll know what's going on with Luis."

Everyone follows me out through the huge sliding doors of the emergency room, around the corner of the building, and back in through the main hospital entrance.

I pause for a minute in the lobby and text Rach, hoping she's holding her phone close.

*U doing OK? I'm here at the hospital with
your mom, aunt, etc.*

Omg, yes. 3rd floor waiting room!

OK, on our way.

"Let's go. She's on the third floor," I say, making my way to the elevators.

We all pile in. The second the doors open on the third floor, Lucca bolts out and heads straight for the waiting room with the rest of us just steps behind. Rach sees her mom and runs straight into her arms.

"Oh, thank you all for coming. The waiting is hell."

"We're here now," says Lucca.

Rach looks up and sees me. "Viv, I'm so sorry about the shower."

"Don't give it another thought. How's Luis? Any word from the doctors yet?"

"No, he's still in surgery. I was told to stay here and that as soon as he's out, the doctor will come and speak to me."

"Okay. Can I get you anything? Are you hungry? Do you want a coffee?"

"I'm not hungry, but coffee does sound good."

"Okay, I'll be right back. Anyone else for coffee?" I ask as I look around the room. Everyone shakes their heads. "Okay, one coffee it is."

I barely get the coffee into Rach's hands when a doctor comes through the door and walks straight towards us. "Are you Luis's family?" he asks.

Rach stands up. "Yes, how is he?"

"His brain was swelling rapidly from the impact he sustained, so it was necessary to remove a small piece of his scalp to make room. We also inserted a drain tube which will remain in place for the next day or two. This will help ensure the pressure doesn't build up again. Controlling this swelling is my main concern. And the next several hours are the most critical. He also had some broken ribs, a fractured left arm, and cracked pelvis. Paramedics told us his left leg was pinned in the crash, and while it wasn't broken, it did need to be stitched up. There were some deep lacerations likely caused by sharp metal under the dashboard. You should expect bruising on his face and limbs to intensify in the next day or two. I will be checking on him regularly and we should know more in a few hours. Right now, all we can do is wait. He's lucky to be alive."

Rach nods. "When can I see him?"

"As soon as we get him moved from the recovery room to a patient room, but only one visitor at a time and please keep those visits brief. He's still unconscious from the surgery. And he won't be moved for at least an hour or two. So, if you want to go get something to eat and come back, you have some time." With that, he turns and walks away.

Rach sits back down. "Thank God he made it through surgery. I thought I'd lost him." Tears slide down her cheeks. Her mom sits beside her, stroking her back and shoulders without speaking a word.

Over an hour passes before they get Luis settled into a patient room, so I decide to run home and grab some of the sandwiches and snacks I made for the shower and bring them back here for everyone. I have a feeling we are in for a long night, and I am right. Even though Rach gets to go in and see Luis, he remains unconscious for the rest of the evening. The nurses reassure Rach this is normal after a brain trauma, and being unconscious is more healing for his brain. But each time she goes into his room, I know all she wants is for him to open his eyes.

After eight o'clock, visiting hours are over, and even though Rach is told she can't visit Luis's room again until the morning, she refuses to leave the hospital. I tell her mom I will stay with her so Lucca and the rest of Rach's family can go home and get some rest.

A little while later, a slender brunette in a volunteer uniform brings us a couple of pillows and blankets and we set up in the waiting room for the night. The nurses know there is no chance Rach is leaving; they don't even try to argue with her.

"Thank you, V, for staying with me; for the food, the coffee, for everything."

"Of course, that's what best friends do. I'm here as long as you need me."

I'm not sure when I dozed off, but when I wake up, I'm alone. It's about five in the morning and I suspect Rach has been allowed back in to see Luis. I fold up the blankets we've used and I'm piling them and our two pillows into a chair when Rach walks back in the room.

"How is he?" I ask.

"Still unconscious."

"Did you get any sleep last night?"

"A little, I think. Thank you again for staying with me."

"Of course. Let me go grab us a coffee. I'll be right back."

When I get back, Rach is on the phone. I presume it's with her mom, as she's telling someone there is no point in them coming back to the hospital this morning. "I'll call if there is any change," she says and hangs up.

"Your mom?" I ask, handing her a coffee.

"Yep. She's always up early and I knew she'd be sitting by the phone waiting for an update. She wanted to come back, but I told her you were here with me. And I'd let her know if anything changes."

"Hey, has anyone reached Luis's parents yet?"

"I've tried, but it's near impossible. They left yesterday on a fourteen-day cruise out of Rome. I sent them an email, but who knows when they will get it. I didn't say too much because I'd rather speak to them on the phone, if possible. Before I freak them out with too many details of what's happening, I thought I'd wait and see what the doctors say today. If things take a turn, and I believe it won't come to that, I could always try reaching out through the cruise line. There is nothing they can do right now, and I hate to shock and worry them when they are so far away. I don't believe Luis would want that either."

"Yeah, probably not. Hopefully, things will improve later today and there won't be a need to reach them."

"Exactly."

Minutes turned into hours, and before we know it, the whole day has passed and there hasn't been any change in Luis. He remains unconscious. I step away a few times briefly to fetch us some more coffee or use the washroom but basically remain at Rach's side the entire day. We still have tons of food, so I offer some to the nurses. They appreciate the gesture.

The announcement over the PA system warns that visiting hours are ending. Rach insists I go home and get some sleep in a real bed. And although I beg her to do the same, I know there is no chance she will. Deciding I'll be more useful to her after a proper night's rest, I agree to leave, but only after her cousin Georgia comes to relieve me.

*

In the morning, I wake up refreshed and ready to get back to the hospital. Before heading out, I pack a small cooler with food for Rach and anyone else who may visit today, along with a couple of thermoses of coffee. I mean, sure, we can get coffee at the hospital, but that doesn't mean it tastes great. Personally, I'm over it.

On the way to the hospital, I stop by Rach's apartment, using the spare key she leaves at my place, to pack up some clean clothes, her toiletries, and her laptop.

Fortunately, Bob is still out of town until tomorrow so I am able to avoid the office and handle any pressing matters remotely. This allows me to spend the entire day at the hospital with Rach, doing my best to comfort her, even though I know the only thing that will do that is Luis waking up. Doctors try their best to reassure her, but admit they were not expecting him to be unconscious this long. So we wait. Another day comes and goes.

"I hate to leave you here, but I have to get back to the office in the morning and should try to grab some sleep. Are you sure you'll be okay tonight?" I ask.

"Yes, I'll be fine. Georgia is working a bit later tonight but promised to pop in as soon as her shift is over. Plus, the nurses said they'd bring up a cot for me tonight so I can sleep in Luis's room. And you brought me everything else I need, so don't worry. I'll call you if there is any change."

Nodding, I give her a hug and head home.

CHAPTER 17

Bob's back and greets me as soon as I get to the office. Little does he know I've already been in for almost two hours. "Hey, good morning! I see everything is in tip-top shape around here."

"Good morning, yes. It's nice to have you back. How was your trip?" I ask.

"Great, but I hear rumours you may be leaving me for a position in Rockhurst's office?"

"Well, yes. It happened rather unexpectedly. But nothing has been decided, at least not that I'm aware of. When I met with Mr. Rockhurst, he told me you spoke very highly of me. I appreciate that."

"I did indeed. You're too bright to be stuck working here forever. You won't be easy to replace, but that will be for me to worry about," Bob says smiling.

"Let's not get ahead of ourselves. I haven't even been offered the job."

"Oh, I'm sure you will be." He winks and walks into his office.

Does Bob know more than he's letting on? I'm sure I'll hear

one way or the other before too long. In the meantime, I've got a lot to keep me busy right here.

Ted walks up to my desk looking fine in his light grey suit and crisp cornflower-blue shirt. "Good morning," he says, all business. "I've got a meeting with Bob this morning, he's expecting me. Okay to go on in?"

I hesitate to answer. His eyes are so blue; I've never noticed how blue before today. Maybe it's his shirt that's making them pop.

"Vivienne, did you hear me?"

"Oh, sorry, Ted. Yes, go right in."

It's half-past nine when I get the call. "Hello, Vivienne. It's Joel Rockhurst calling." As if I wouldn't recognize his voice.

"Good morning, Mr. Rockhurst."

"I'm calling because we've concluded all our interviews, and I would like to officially offer you the position as my executive assistant."

"Wow, that's great! I'm honoured. Thank you, sir."

"Carolyn is going to email you the offer, including the compensation plan. Look it over, and don't hesitate to call me if you have any questions. If at all possible, I'd like your answer by tomorrow morning."

"Yes, of course. Thank you."

"You're welcome. I do hope you'll accept. I think we'd work well together."

"Thank you again," I say as I hang up the phone.

I can hardly believe it. I open my email, but nothing has come in. Who am I kidding, it's not like I really need to look over anything. Of course I'm going to take the position.

I text Rach to share the news.

Hey, how's Luis?
Thought u could use some good news.
Rockhurst called—I got the job! I'll come to the

*hospital after work. Should I pick up dinner
on the way?*

Rach texts back immediately:

*That's fantastic! So proud of you!
No change here. Yes please, dinner sounds
great.*

No matter what life throws at Rach, she's still my biggest supporter.

After work, I do as promised and pick up some dinner on the way back to the hospital. Rach is keeping herself occupied on her laptop when I arrive.

"Hey, I'm back, and I brought burgers and fries. Thought you could use some comfort food."

"Hi, yeah, that sounds good. Thank you."

"I'm guessing there's still no change with Luis?"

"Nope. The nurse is in with him now, checking his vitals and switching his IV bags," she says, grabbing a couple of French fries from the bag and stuffing them in her mouth.

"Hard to believe it's been over seventy-two hours already since his accident. Did you get any sleep last night?" I ask as I look around. "What time did Georgia leave?"

"She left before noon. She had some things to take care of and, honestly, she wasn't helping. All she did was pace back and forth. I was sure she would leave a wear pattern on the floor if she hung around here any longer."

I unwrap my burger and take a bite. "So, what have you been doing since she left?"

"There's not much to do. I spoke to my mom a couple of times and wandered down to the cafeteria to grab a Greek chicken salad for lunch. But other than that, I'm waiting, hoping Luis will show us some sign he's still in there. The doctors finally did admit to me today that he is actually in a coma. They said it could be days, weeks, or even months before he wakes up. I'm choosing to believe it's going to be days and I'm hoping he knows I'm here. It's so strange, talking to him and not getting any response, not even a flicker…"

"I've heard people in comas can hear and are aware of what goes on around them."

"Me too, that's why I won't give up on him. I know if the situation was reversed, he'd be here talking to me, encouraging me to fight. I'll continue to do the same for him."

"You're amazing, Rach."

"That's what the nurses keep telling me. Enough about that. You got the job! That's fantastic. Tell me everything."

"Well, Mr. Rockhurst wants me to let him know by tomorrow, but my mind was made up before I even opened the email."

"You got the offer by email? Gosh, you'd think he'd have at least phoned you."

"Oh, he did. He had the official offer put in writing and emailed to me following his call."

"That makes sense, I guess. How do you think Bob will take the news?"

"He told me I was too good to stay in my current position forever, and while I'll be hard to replace, he didn't want me to worry about that. He sounded happy for me. Almost as if he knew before I did."

"Do you think he did?"

"Not sure, but I guess it doesn't matter. In the email I received, it says they want me to start as soon as possible. Carolyn is hoping to spend some time training me before she leaves and I gather the sooner the better for her."

"Well, you deserve it. You bust your butt for that place; it's nice to see your hard work has paid off." Rach crumples up the wrapper from her burger and tosses it into the garbage can. "I'm going to go check in with Luis for a bit. Do you want to hang around for a while?"

"Absolutely, you go ahead. I'll be here when you come out."

While Rach is in visiting with Luis, I finish my burger and call up the job offer I saved to my phone and re-read it. I type up my acceptance letter and save it to my drafts. Think I'll wait until at least eleven tomorrow morning before responding so I don't seem overly eager. Then I type up an email to Bob, letting him know I've been officially offered the position in Rockhurst's office and ask how I might be able to help in sourcing or training my replacement. The email is more difficult to write than I expected. I've grown rather attached to Bob over the last couple of years and must admit I will miss working with him.

Rach returns to the waiting room forty-five minutes later, wiping tears from her face.

"You okay?" I ask.

"Yeah. I'm okay." She's a good liar.

"Do you still have those old reruns of *Friends* on your laptop?" I ask.

"Yes."

"I thought we could watch a couple of episodes before I have to head out." I'm thinking a little light-hearted comedy couldn't hurt right now, and Rach obviously agrees with me. She proceeds to grab her laptop out of her bag and open it up.

A few minutes later, during a ridiculous scene where Joey gets a turkey stuck on his head, Rach starts to laugh, cry, and then laugh some more until I can't tell whether she's laughing or crying. "Are you okay?" I ask again, handing her a tissue.

"Yes. I so needed this." She giggles. "Thank you, V, for always knowing what I need."

The rest of the week is pretty much the same. I get up early, go to work, then either run back home and prepare dinner for Rach or pick up something on the way back to the hospital.

Either way, that's where I end up: at the hospital, spending my evenings with Rach.

Tonight is different. I arrive to find her surrounded by family who has brought in all kinds of homemade dishes. Rach laughs at something funny Maria said and Lucca dishes up her famous pastelón, which is to die for. I stay long enough to enjoy a piece and a quick visit, but then decide to head home and take a long hot bath.

Back at my apartment, I make sure to acknowledge that I don't do this often enough. Take time for myself, that is. Truthfully, I can't remember the last time I decided to shut out the world and experience some quiet solitude. I pour myself a glass of wine, turn the ringer off on my phone, dim the lights, and light my favourite rose-scented candle.

Stepping into the bath, the image of the psychic woman strangely pops into my head along with her warning to put more balance into my life. What is wrong with me? Why do I have such a desire to always try to control things, fix things, change them, even improve them? Other women must feel a similar overwhelming need to always be in control, right? I sink down until my chin is resting in the water and allow the warmth to envelop me. Answers don't immediately come to me, but for once, I'm in no rush.

I lift my head to take a sip of wine and add a little more hot water to the tub before sinking back down again. Wrapped in bubbles, I close my eyes and all the pent up tension in my muscles releases. My arms float weightlessly at my sides and my mind begins to quiet. This time is a gift I'm giving myself.

***

Though I still pop into the hospital from time to time, I don't feel the need to stay as long as I did before. Rach's family seems to have things covered. Even the occasional trips to her apartment to pick up whatever she needs are being handled by Lucca, Maria, or her cousins now.

On top of that, Rach has become friendly with all of Luis's regular nurses and they've gone above and beyond to make her comfortable. They've even allowed her to use the shower in Luis's room whenever she feels the need to freshen up. Fortunately for Rach, she had several weeks of vacation time saved up, a time I'm certain was for her honeymoon. Nevertheless, it allows her to remain at the hospital without having to worry about work.

As for my own work, Bob has a niece, Samatha, with an administrative background and he's decided to bring her on board as my replacement. She has a bubbly personality and is super eager to please. After a few days of training her, I can already tell she'll be an asset to Bob. Turns out he's going to be fine without me. Gotta admit that while I'm thrilled Bob has someone as competent as Samatha on his team, I was taken back a bit by the speed at which I've been replaced.

Seems it's now plausible for me to step out of my current position and into my new one next week. Before I leave on Friday afternoon, Bob calls me into his office. "Well, Vivienne, Samantha tells me you've done a fine job training her this week, and I appreciate that."

"Honestly, I think you've found a good one. She's going to do a great job, I'm sure of it."

"I want to thank you for all your hard work," Bob says as he pulls an envelope from his top drawer and slides it across his desk towards me. "A little something from all of us."

Inside the envelope is a card signed with well-wishes from everyone in the department along with five hundred dollars cash. "Wow, sir, thank you, but you didn't have to do that. It's too much."

"Not at all. We wanted to. Your dedication to me and this department has been immeasurable. Buy yourself a new outfit or something for your new job." He comes around from behind his desk and gives me a hug and as he pulls back, he says, "You'll be missed Vivienne, but you won't be far so don't be a stranger. Pop in and say hi every once in a while, okay?"

"Will do. Thank you."

It's a bit odd walking out this early on a Friday afternoon, but Bob reassures me there is nothing left for me to do. And I told him a week ago there was a personal matter I need to attend to today. I head back out to my desk to collect the last of my things, I pause for a moment and look around, taking it all in one last time before I walk towards the elevators.

On my way home, I visit my doctor's office for a quick checkup. I've already postponed this appointment three times, so I figure I'd better not miss this one. Height, weight, blood pressure, a couple of vials of blood, and my annual pap smear. Oh, joy. I've never met a woman who isn't a least a little squeamish as the doctor gloves up, instructs her to put her feet together, knees apart, and relax. Relax? Privates spread open like a turkey ready to be stuffed Thanksgiving morning. Yeah, sure, okay. Relax. Got it.

"That's it, Vivienne, we're all done here," my doctor announces as he stands to leave the room. "We'll call you if there are any issues once we get your test results back."

"So, no news is good news then," I awkwardly reply as I adjust my paper gown and swing my legs over the side of the examining table.

CHAPTER 18

Carolyn Gauge is ready and waiting for me when I arrive Monday morning at nine. She wastes no time showing me around, acquainting me with Mr. Rockhurst's schedule and bringing me up to speed with everything I need to know. And, it's a lot. Fortunately for me, Carolyn keeps impeccable records and has already created flow charts I can refer to should questions arise. She will be staying on for the next five days to help with the transition.

The office is quite upscale compared to I-Sales. Here, floor to ceiling windows floods the space with natural light which bounces off the polished porcelain-tile floor. The waiting area is expansive, but a large vintage rug with a soft floral pattern helps to define the space. On top of the rug is a contemporary white-leather seating arrangement, and in the center is a large glass coffee table with bevelled edges and polished chrome legs. A collection of magazines is neatly fanned out on the table together with a large silver vase holding an elegant display of fresh flowers. A rich, grey wooden side table with chrome accents rests against the wall, complete with a hot beverage station. There appears to be a wide selection of self-serve coffees and teas and a tray of freshly baked goods which I saw the staff placing out when I arrived this morning.

Carolyn catches me looking in that direction. "Every couple of days, a local florist switches the floral arrangement for a new one and each morning, staff from a nearby bakery deliver fresh cookies, squares, and donuts. Our own cleaning staff will freshen up the station each night and restock the coffees and teas, and also ensure fresh milk and cream are in the small refrigerator. So you won't need to worry about any of that. Mr. Rockhurst likes to ensure his guests are well taken care of. You are welcome to help yourself as well."

"Good morning, Vivienne, Carolyn," says Mr. Rockhurst as he strolls out of his office and up to Carolyn's desk. Technically, I guess it's my desk too.

"Good morning, sir. Carolyn was just getting me acquainted with your schedule."

"Wonderful. Carolyn, be sure to bring Vivienne up to speed about next Saturday. I'm stepping out for a few minutes but shouldn't be long, and I have my cell if you need me."

"Sure thing, Mr. Rockhurst," said Carolyn. "And don't worry about next Saturday, we have that covered."

"I know you do," he says, smiling.

As soon as he's out of sight, I turn to Carolyn and ask, "What is happening next Saturday?"

"Mr. Rockhurst is holding an event at his home for all JetStreams' major clients and a half dozen potential new clients he hopes to reel in. He's pulling out all the stops. Much of the planning has already been done, but you and I will be spending the next few days on little else."

"Wow, okay. How many people is he expecting?"

"A little north of one hundred, including some current JetStream executives and their spouses. But don't worry, we'll spend the rest of the morning going over the usual and then we'll get onto the plans for Saturday.

I nod as Carolyn guides my attention back to the computer screen. She goes over all Mr. Rockhurst's files, making sure I understand her digital filing system and how to retrieve important documents and memos. The system isn't organized that different from how we did it in I-Sales, so everything seems rather intuitive to me.

The rest of the day goes smoothly; well, other than the moment I accidentally disconnect Mr. Rockhurst's mother. I am mortified, but he seems more entertained than upset, saying she'll get over it. And although we don't get any planning for next Saturday's party accomplished, that is first on our agenda for tomorrow. It was a productive first day.

Walking towards the elevator, I pull my phone out and see a text from Rach. It came through over an hour ago.

*He moved his hand today! The doctors think
he might actually be starting to come out of it!*

I text back:

That's great! Just finished work. On my way!

Room 326, she replies.

When I get to the hospital, I head straight for Luis's room. Though it's been weeks since the accident, I haven't seen Luis yet. But I knew if he was regaining consciousness, Rach wouldn't leave his side. Waiting outside would be futile.

As I walk through the heavy doors separating the waiting area from the patient rooms, my nostrils become invaded by the pungent smell of antiseptic and urine. As I go down the corridor, nurses zigzag between the rooms ahead of me. Hampers overflowing with old towels and bedding appear abandoned in the hall. I can hear low whispers, muffled moans, and cries from patients' rooms, and the consistent beeping of machines as I scan the numbers for Luis's. A nurse pushing an old man in a wheelchair exits one of the rooms in front of me, nodding as she passes by in the opposite direction. I see room 326.

Rounding the corner into Luis's room, I find curtains drawn around the bed. They don't quite reach the floor, allowing me to see Rach's feet folded beneath the legs of a chair pushed up tight to the side of the bed. I whisper her name as I draw back the corner of the curtain, but she doesn't hear me. She is resting her head on the edge of the mattress with Luis's hand in hers.

Luis lies there, eyes closed, IV bags and monitors filling the space near the head of the bed. He has white bandages on his skull and his left arm is in a cast, but there is no sign of a breathing machine or mask on his face, which I'd been prepared to see. I lean forward and gently touch Rach on the shoulder. She turns around and smiles at me.

"You're here!"

"Yes. He looks good. I thought you said he was on a breathing machine?"

"He was, but they removed it earlier this afternoon. He's breathing on his own now. He even opened his eyes slightly, but he hasn't spoken yet. The doctors don't want to rush it, but said if he hasn't come around on his own by tonight, they will give him a little nudge—whatever that means. Can you believe it, V? He's coming back to me!"

I lean down and give her a hug. "It's amazing."

He's in a semi-private room but the curtains are drawn around the other bed, so it's unclear whether it's occupied. There are fresh flowers on the windowsill and what appears to be a bath bomb on Luis's nightstand.

"Is that a bath bomb?" I ask.

"Yes, I found it in the hospital gift shop. It's fragrant in a good way and helps mask some of the unpleasant hospital smells. I don't want the first thing Luis smells when he wakes up to be rubbing alcohol and urine."

"Well, it appears to be working. It smells better here than it does out in the hallway. So, can I get you anything? I didn't take time to stop on the way, but could head back out and grab you some dinner now, or maybe a coffee?"

"No, I'm okay for a bit, but thanks."

There's a light tap on the door. Luis's doctor strolls in and walks up to his bed.

"How's Luis doing tonight?" he asks.

"He moved his fingers a few times and opened his eyes briefly once or twice since you were last in," Rach replies.

"Well, I think it's time to see how he'll respond to some stimuli," the doctor says as he pulls back the sheets from the end of the bed. He runs the back of a pen up and down the bottoms of Luis's feet while watching to see if there is any response. And there is: movement. Luis's feet respond, and he opens his eyes, albeit only slightly.

"That's good," says the doctor.

"Luis, honey, can you hear me?" Luis's eyes open a little more. "He hears me!" Rach stands and leans in closer as the doctor covers Luis's feet and moves up the side of the bed towards his head.

"It appears as if he does," says the doctor. "Welcome back, Luis. Can you blink once for me if you can hear us?"

Luis blinks. "Oh, my God! Did you see that?" Rach can barely contain her excitement.

"Yes. That's wonderful. Now, can you try to follow my finger, Luis?" says the doctor as he proceeds to move his finger from side to side in front of Luis's eyes and then up and down from the bridge of his nose to the top of his lip.

Luis's eyes do exactly as they are instructed. The doctor nods approvingly and says, "You've been asleep for quite a while and we've only just removed your breathing tube this morning, so I'd like you to take it slow. But if you can, I'd like you to try to speak."

Rach lifts his hand off the bed and whispers, "You can do this, Luis. I know you can."

Luis's eyes fix on Rach, and he lets out a weak, "Hi, Bebe."

Rach's emotions flood to the surface, tears stream down her cheeks as her whole face lights up. "Hi. Welcome back! I've missed you," she responds, clutching his hand tightly.

"How are you feeling? Any pain?" the doctor asks him.

Luis shakes his head but doesn't take his eyes off Rach. "How long have I been out?" he asks.

"Weeks. It's been weeks."

Rach barely responds when the doctor asks if we'd both mind stepping out of the room for a few minutes so he can examine Luis. "I'll be quick, then you can visit a bit longer before I recommend we let Luis get some rest."

"Okay, we'll be right outside." Rach lowers Luis's hand back to the bed and leans down to kiss him on the cheek before she turns to follow me out of the room.

We are no sooner in the hall than she throws her arms around me, squealing in delight. "He's awake! I'm so excited, he's awake!"

"I can see that," I say as a little laugh escapes my lips. Her giddiness is infectious.

"I *knew* he'd come back. I just knew it!"

"I couldn't be happier for you. You've been a trooper this whole time. Camping out here, being by his side day in and day out… You never gave up on him."

"How much longer is the doctor going to take?" she asks, pacing the floor.

"I'm sure he'll be out any minute now. I'd like to give you and Luis a bit of privacy. Maybe now is a good time for me to go grab us some dinner."

"Oh, sure, okay. Thank you. It means a lot to me that you've been here to support me. I don't know what I'd do without you." A single tear drops onto her cheek as she continues. "I couldn't ask for a better friend, truly."

I take a wet wipe out of my purse and clean Rach's face with it. Her make-up is long gone, but the blackened streaks of her mascara remain. "I feel the same about you."

An hour later, I return with our dinner to find Rach's entire family in the waiting room. They are all smiling and laughing.

"Hey, sweetie. Did you hear the news about Luis?" Lucca asks as I enter the room.

"Yes, I was here earlier. I went back out to grab Rach some dinner."

"Oh, she didn't tell me that and I just took her in a huge plate of food."

"No, worries. I'll have extra for lunch tomorrow. Think it's okay to go in and say a quick hello?"

"Yes, of course, we were just giving them a few minutes to themselves."

As I walk in his room, I see Luis sitting up and talking. He and Rach are deep in conversation, and don't notice me until I'm right beside the bed.

"Luis, you look great. It's wonderful to see you awake. How do you feel? Can I give you a hug?"

"Sure, I won't break. Not anymore anyway. I feel pretty good, considering." Luis hugs me back. "Rachel tells me you've been here with her every night since the accident."

Rach smiles but doesn't take her eyes off Luis. "You've been my guardian angel, V."

"Well, I'm not certain it's been every night." I've come to realize that as much as I want to do it all, be in control of every situation, I don't need to be. Rach is fine, she's been fine. She has so many other people who love and support her. "I saw your family out in the waiting room. When did they arrive?"

"Oh, about thirty minutes ago. I know you went out to pick up dinner but you know my mom, she had to bring in a ton of food." Rach looks up, pointing her chin in the direction of the stacked Tupperware containers. "Luis's nurse told us he can try to eat something if he feels up to it, so they are bringing him up a tray in a few minutes. They prefer he starts out slow. Guess they think mom's empanadillas and alcapurrias might be a bit rich for his first meal." She lets out a little laugh.

"Well, I think you two should enjoy your meal without a third wheel hovering around. I'm going to take my dinner and head home. I don't want to intrude, and if I'm being honest, I'm getting tired." I place my hand on Luis's right arm. "It's great to see you feeling better, Luis. We've missed you."

"Thanks, it's good to be back."

"Thanks again, V, for everything," Rach says. "I'll call you tomorrow."

"Sounds good." I wave goodbye over my shoulder as I head out the door.

On the drive home, I can't help but think how lucky Luis is to make such a remarkable recovery, and how happy he and Rach looked tonight. I'm sure their relationship will be stronger because of this ordeal, and I imagine as soon as Luis is up to it, the wedding plans will get back on track.

These few weeks have shown me how life moves forward regardless. It's impossible to control every situation and trying to do so is exhausting, and futile. Things have a way of working themselves out. I don't have to be Wonder Woman. Sure, I will always work hard at whatever I do, but I'm realizing it's all right to let others take the reins sometimes.

After I park the car, I grab the dinner bag from the seat beside me and head up to my apartment. I reach the third floor and peer down the hallway. *Who is that?* I take a couple of steps closer and gasp. No, it's not possible. I stand with locked knees; my keys and dinner bag slip from my hands. The noise of them hitting the floor draws attention from the dark figure outside my apartment door. He lifts his head towards me and stands.

"Vivey!"

"Oh my God!" *Am I seeing things?*

He walks towards me. My feet stay glued in place. When he reaches me, he bends and picks up the keys and dinner bag off the floor. I can't speak; it's as if I'm looking at a ghost.

"Are you okay?" Danny asks.

"I—I—don't understand. What are you doing here? Is this even real?"

Danny chuckles, grabs my hand, raising it to his lips, and softly kisses it. "Yes, this is real. I'm back." He picks up my keys and bag. "I've been doing a lot of self-reflection lately..."

"You and me both," I add.

"I've made a decision and I needed to see you."

"What decision?"

"Let's go inside and I'll tell you." His eyes fall to my neck. "You're wearing the locket I gave you."

"Yes," I respond, reaching up to touch it. I stop short of telling him it's the only necklace I wear now and ask, "How long have you been waiting here?" I'm still trying to process this is actually happening.

With my hand still in his, Danny guides me to my apartment door, unlocks it and leads me inside, closing the door behind us.

"My flight got in a few hours ago and I came straight here."

"Why didn't you tell me you were coming home?"

"There was no time."

"You could have texted."

"Does that really matter now? I'm here."

"No, no, it doesn't matter." I wrap my arms around him and cover his face in kisses.

"So you *are* happy to see me," he chuckles.

"Yes, delighted. I'm just shocked. You're the last person I would have expected to find waiting on my doorstep."

"Oh, yeah, who else would you have been expecting?"

"No one. You know what I mean. Okay, so tell me, what is this decision you've made?"

Danny pulls me to the couch. "Vivey, these last few months away from you were harder than I imagined. I realized I don't want us to be apart. I don't want you to move on. What I want is for us to be together."

"I want that too."

"I don't know what the future looks like, but I'd like for us to figure it out together. I love you, and I'm hoping you still love me?" His eyebrows rise as he anticipates my answer.

"Of course I still love you."

"You understand going to Saudi wasn't about leaving you, but about trying to provide for my son, right?"

"Yes, I know, but that doesn't mean it didn't hurt me when you left."

"It hurt me too, and that's why I had to come back. I don't have everything worked out yet and I know things won't be easy. I'll probably need two or three jobs to make up for what I could have made had I stayed in Saudi. And that means things might be a little crazy at times—but it can be *our* crazy." He pauses for a moment to take a deep breath, his eyes staring intently into mine. "I'm so sorry I hurt you, Vivey. That was never my intention."

There is no time for me to respond or prepare myself before Danny slides off the couch and onto one knee. "If you'll have me, I'd like to spend the rest of my life making it up to you."

My heart races and I cover my mouth with my hand in a weak attempt to mask my surprise. Is this really happening? He pulls a small velvety box out of his pocket, opens it and slides it towards me, revealing a sparkling diamond solitaire atop a rose-coloured band.

"It's not as spectacular as you deserve, but it's...."

"Perfect, it's perfect."

He removes the ring from the box and takes my left hand in his. "Vivienne Ramsey, will you spend forever with me, as my partner, my wife?"

"Yes. Of course, I will!" I can feel the goosebumps running up and down my arms.

He slides the ring onto my finger and climbs back on the couch beside me. Placing his hands on either side of my face, he presses his lips to mine. "I love you, Vivey."

"I can't believe this—did we just get engaged?" I ask while admiring how the light bounces off my ring.

"I believe we did," Danny says, smiling.

I drop my head back against the top of the couch. "Wow, what a day this has been. I have so much to tell you. So much has happened while you've been away. I don't even know where to start."

"Well, how about we grab a drink to celebrate our engagement and you start at the beginning? I have a few things to share with you too," he adds.

"Sure, and Danny..."

"Yeah?"

"This time, I promise to let you take the lead." I smile and wink. "Sometimes."

One week later, Danny's employer dissolved all three-year contracts due to the rise in violence in Saudi Arabia. Danny and others who had loyally served three months or more with the company were allowed to keep their hefty signing bonuses. His bonus, along with the profit he'd made selling his house, allowed him to catch up on all of Nick's medical bills. Sure, Danny was near broke again, but it was worth it.

The tensions of Vivienne and Danny's past faded to a distant memory as they planned their future. Danny reached out to his old boss at The Rail and secured his previous position. And with his first paycheque, he kept the promise he made to his son and the three of them returned to the zoo to visit the wolves Nick so adores.

Danny also returned to work at JetStream and was swiftly promoted to head mechanic. His new position came with a nice pay bump and allowed him to drop his late-night job at The Rail a few months later. Meanwhile, Vivienne continues to help steer the ship at JetStream as Joel Rockhurst's executive assistant, a job she loves.

Fourteen months after their engagement, Danny and Vivienne were married in a small chapel on the outskirts of Savannah with a few of their closest family and friends in attendance. Rach, with her protruding belly and radiant pre-baby glow, stood as Vivienne's maid of honour. Her husband, Luis, who made a full and complete recovery following his accident, stood next to Danny as his best man. Nick was there too, of course, beaming from ear to ear all decked out in a dark grey suit and tie. He carried the happy couple's wedding bands in a special wooden box Danny had made etched with the words *His and Hers* on top.

Nick underwent his final heart procedure, successfully and without complication, just in time to pick his room in the three-bedroom, two-storey house Danny and Vivienne closed on, right outside the city limits. The downpayment and closing costs for their new home were paid for out of Vivienne's inheritance, something they know in their hearts Big Mike would have encouraged. Vivienne and Danny couldn't be happier knowing that his memory will always be a part of the new family they've created.

The Goat finally came out of storage and found its place in their oversized garage next to Danny's motorcycle. And the big backyard longs for future children, and maybe even a wolf-looking dog to come and play. Vivienne and Danny agree that they won't wait too long before making Nick a big brother, a fact that excites Rach and Luis who aren't shy about reminding the couple the fun they'll have raising their kids together.

Their life is crazy and full of love, but it's the type of forever crazy that Vivenne dreamed of, Danny promised, and they choreographed together.

ABOUT THE AUTHOR

Jennifer Nolan is an award winning author who began her publishing career over two decades ago. During this time, she has written more than twenty non-fiction titles that stretch across multiple genres.

Taking a leap into the world of fiction, Nolan masterfully pens this contemporary romance in a style all her own. Successfully creating compelling characters with real, everyday problems resulting in an unforgettable debut novel.

Our Forever Crazy Love takes place in the beautiful town of Savannah, Georgia, far from the author's own home in Ontario, Canada where she resides with her husband of almost thirty years.

Jennifer loves hearing from her readers and she can be reached at jennifernolanbooks@gmail.com